A Little Dogs Prayer.   Author Jan McCulloch

Part One

Chapter One

I leapt on the bed and woke up the twins by licking their faces and wriggling all over them until they squirmed and giggled and pushed me away. Then I scooted off downstairs ready to be let out into the garden. The air was fresh, a touch of autumn blowing on the breeze and the sparkle of dew drops on the grass. I charged out and raced around the garden sniffing at the ground to see who had visited in my absence. Birds. Hedgehog. Toad. SQUIRREL! I knew it! Despite a thorough search of the bushes and a good look up into the trees, he was nowhere to be seen. I would get him next time! I heard my name being called so I hurried back up to the house for breakfast.

The twins were almost ready for school. I knew it was a school day because they had different clothes to the ones they wore to play in. I liked the non-school days best because the twins were fun and played with me. Especially Jade, she was my favourite because she was so kind and sneaked me treats when no one was looking. Ellie was fun most of the time but she liked teasing me and was sometimes a little bit cruel. She liked to dress me up in silly clothes and did not play the games a little dog enjoys. But School days were okay too because I always went along with mum and dad to drop off the twins at the school gates before being taken for a walk in the park or by the river.

As soon as the twins had put on their coats I ran to find my special ball and danced around them until Jade managed to catch me and put my lead on. It was a routine I loved! And so did they. The twins giggled and called me silly names while I danced and wagged my tail furiously.

Once we got to the car I knew it was time to settle down. Brian and Jean, the twin's parents, mostly known as mum and dad, suffered no nonsense from myself or the twins once we got in. I was in my own comfortable crate with a fleece blanket in the back, and the twins put on their seat belts without being told. Jade turned around and pushed her fingers through the side of the crate so I could lick them. I knew she loved me more than anyone else. I loved looking out of the windows as we drove along to the school. Panting and wagging my tail in excitement when I saw other dogs being walked.

Once the twins had climbed out of the car and said their goodbyes, I knew it was almost time for my morning run. Park or riverbank? I never knew which one it would be until we got there, but I enjoyed them both. This morning it was the river bank. Lovely smells and long grass and a pebbled slope down to the river that allowed me to paddle in the cool water and have a drink if I wished.

Brian and Jean were not as much fun as the twins. They didn't throw my ball or play silly games, but I enjoyed our walks and this morning was no exception. It was a long walk and I was free to run around and investigate all the exciting scents.

Once back in the car, I felt a strange aura coming from both Brian and Jean. It was a sadness. Or some sort of regret. I couldn't work out which.

Jean was stroking my head gently and I could feel her unhappiness. I was worried I had done something wrong, like the time I pretended her slipper was a squirrel and killed it dead! But this was a different sort of sadness.

And Brian seemed guilty and would not look at me. They shut my crate and got into the car. I was worried but still eager to get home to see if the squirrel was in the garden. I was sure I would get him this time!

Once home Jean did not take my lead off as she usually did when we went into the garden. I didn't get the chance to see if the squirrel was back! Instead, I was taken straight into the house. Jean brushed me and dried my legs while the Brian went up to the bedroom. After my brush, Jean clipped on my lead and shouted upstairs to Brian but he did not reply. Again, I felt her sadness. A very deep sadness that made me want to howl.

I walked with Jean back to the car. I was very worried now. She was so sad that her eyes were watering. I had seen this happen to the twins when they hurt themselves, but this was different. She was full of grief and was shaking while silent tears poured down her face. She put me into the car and I tried to lick her tears away but she wouldn't let me. It seemed to make her worse and she started to sob.

I saw her run back into the house and a few moments later Brian came out and got into the car. He didn't look at me or speak. He drove away from the house and I could feel the guilt pouring out of him. I sighed and lay down on my fleece blanket with my nose on my paws. I didn't feel like looking out of the windows and I didn't wag my tail. I felt that something was wrong. Very wrong.

The journey was not a long one. The car stopped in a large car park and Brian got out but he didn't come to put my lead on, he just stood smoking a cigarette. Within a few minutes another car arrived and I was lifted out of my crate. Brian did not look at me or pat me. He handed me to a stranger and after a brief exchange he strode away. The stranger put me into a very small, dirty crate in the back of the strange car. I was up on my back legs, trying to see where Brian was going. What was happening? Why was I in this strange car with all these strange smells? I started to whine …. Small cries to get his attention so he would come back. But the stranger whacked his hand on the side of the crate and yelled at me to be quiet. I shook with fear as he slammed the doors shut. The car smelled of fear too. All the strange scents of very many dogs who had been in here before me, afraid, just as I was.

A Little Dogs Prayer.   Author Jan McCulloch

Chapter Two

The journey was a long one. There were no windows in this car. I heard the stranger singing along to music as he drove. His voice sounded strange. An unusual lilt to his words that was unlike any voice I had ever heard before. After a long while the car stopped and another dog was put into a crate next to me. This dog was already shaking with terror and her eyes were bulging out of her head. She was covered in her own excrement and her fur was stained orange from urine around her tail and back legs. She cowered at the back of her crate and would not even come to touch noses with me. When I wagged my tail at the stranger he took no notice.

After another long while on the road I was desperate for the toilet. I whined and tried to let the stranger know what I wanted, but he yelled and struck the crate again so fiercely that I wet myself in fright. The shock, on top of an already full bladder, was too much for me. The other poor dog in the crate next to me did the same and the acrid smell of our urine filled the air.

When the car stopped again I was hoping we would be let out this time. But instead, another dog joined us. This dog went into a crate stacked above us, and this dog was seriously aggressive! Snarling and snapping and trying to savage the people who were handling her. Her coat was matted and her tummy looked swollen. Her eyes were sore and her nails were very long. One of the strangers had a pole and a noose which he used to throw her bodily into the crate. Such was her distress she messed herself and diarrhoea dripped from her crate down onto me and my neighbour. The stench was horrendous. Her anal glands had evacuated their contents too, a smell that screamed to our instincts of a terror so great that we trembled and pushed ourselves as far to the back of our crates as we possibly could. The people threw a bucket of strong disinfectant into the crate to swill out the mess, not caring that it burned our eyes and inflamed our sensitive nostrils.

The inside of the car was too hot and the smell was almost unbearable. The people did not seem to notice. There were two of them now. They called each other Jock and Sean. As we drove on, they laughed and smoked and ignored us completely. The dog above me occasionally emitted a low growl in her throat.

When the car stopped again after what seemed an eternity, we welcomed the fresh air as the doors were opened briefly. A box was lifted into the car and shoved up against the front of my crate. The whimpering that came from within told us that there were puppies inside. The dog above, previously vicious and snarling, came to the front of the crate and whined softly to them, making them all cry louder and scramble up the sides of the box. Jock, the bigger of the two strangers, lifted a couple of pups out of the box and pushed them into the crate with her. I could hear her licking them and they fell silent, so he put the rest of the pups in with her too.

Seven pups. Dirty and running with fleas, pot bellies that were full of worms. Bony little bodies with no spare puppy fat. All of them giving off the scent of fear, despite their young age.

The crate was small so there was very little room to move but I could hear them snuffling and settling down. They must have been exhausted and were grateful for the comfort of a warm tongue licking them to sleep.

The rest of the journey was uneventful. It was dark outside when the car travelled over rough ground that bumped us around. The puppies started to whimper. At last the car stopped. Jock and Sean got out. No one opened the back doors. We heard their footsteps retreating and then a door opened and closed. Silence. The temperature in the car started to drop. We were soon shivering after being cramped and hot for so long. My throat ached with thirst. We heard owls hoot, and the distant call of a fox. We all lay huddled in our own mess. The puppies cried fitfully in their sleep. I thought about home and the twins. Especially Jade. And my warm bed by the radiator. What kind of hell was this?

As daylight filled the car and the birds started singing we became restless and shuffled around in our crates. The puppies were weak with hunger and tried to suckle from the dog they shared the crate with but she had nothing for them. They whimpered and she licked them until they slept again, their bony little bodies twitching when the fleas sucked their blood. I was already itching. Fleas had jumped onto me and were having a feast! I scratched until I bled.

The sun was filtering through the trees when we heard voices. Jock and Sean came and opened the doors. Despite myself, I wagged my tail in greeting. They took no notice. Our crates were lifted out into the fresh autumn air. One by one we were lifted roughly out of the cages and carried into a building, except for the aggressive dog with the pups she was caring for. Her whole crate was carried into the building and she was tipped out into a small pen next to me, and the puppies were carried away. She screamed after them and threw herself at the bars of the pen until she was exhausted. The building was dark, lit only by a few skylight windows covered in cobwebs. The air was cool and stale, but thankfully there was a bowl of water. The bowl itself was rusty and coated in green slime and the water was rank and covered in scum but such was my thirst I drank every drop.

As my eyes became adjusted to the dim surroundings, I could see there were rows of kennels on either side of the building we were in. Some forty or more altogether, each containing at least one dog, though some pens had three or four very young dogs housed together. The floor was concrete with a light dusting of sawdust and there was an old wooden pallet to sit on. Most of the other kennel floors were covered in mess that had not been cleaned up and all the dogs were filthy. None of them barked. They all hid at the back of their kennels. Even the very young dogs. There was an overwhelming feeling of dread in this place. When the Jock and Sean returned to top up our water bowls, they used a tin watering can to bring stagnant rain water from an old water butt in a corner where the roof leaked. None of us ventured to the front of our kennels. We sat silently at the back, in the shadows. Then Sean brought food in a wheel barrow. No dishes. Just a handful of dried food thrown onto the floor. I did not touch it. Nor did the other new arrivals. But I saw other residents eating ravenously as soon as he was gone.

There was a dog opposite me who stood and licked the bars of her kennel for hours. The dog next to her was chewing her own tail until it was raw. They hardly stopped to eat or drink or sleep. It seemed to be an obsession that they had no control over. Their eyes looked blank and they seemed unaware of their surroundings. It made me shudder and I could not bear to watch.

My first day here was ending. Darkness was falling and with it, the rustling and squeaking of the night creatures. I saw strange long tailed animals scurrying along the beams in the roof and lurking behind the water butt. Their eyes glowed red in the dark. In shape and size, they reminded me of the squirrel back home, though unlike him they had an evil musky smell. The smell enraged me and had me frantically scrabbling at the bars, barking and yelping in frustration when I could not get to them. A light shone through the building Jock came in, carrying a torch.

He saw me desperately trying to get to the night creatures but instead of letting me out to pursue the beasts, I found myself being beaten black and blue, thrown around the kennel until I felt every bone in my body must be broken. I quivered in terror at the back of the kennel as he slammed the door and left. I had learned why all the other dogs in the building were silent. After that day, I never barked again.

The following days were much the same. Jock or Sean came into the building only once a day, unless any of us a made a noise. One night, a dog in a kennel close to mine started howling. She was a poor timid creature who had not eaten for days. She was wearing a collar like mine so I guessed she had not been here long. The other dogs did not have collars, or if they did they were hidden under filthy matted fur. Within minutes of her starting to howl Jock arrived with his torch. I was terrified in case he thought it was me making the noise. He walked slowly up and down the kennels, then took a big stick and started banging it back and forth across all the bars. The noise was deafening! We were all shaking in terror before he left, and the little dog who had been howling was silent.

A few days later I heard children playing outside. I was on my feet in a second! I did not recognise their voices but my experiences with children had always been happy ones. I missed the twins so much. I could hear these children bouncing a ball and running around just outside the building. I whimpered softly, afraid to bark but so eager to see those children and to be able to run and play with them. As their voices faded away and I realised I could not get out, a new kind of desolation washed over me. I lay on the filthy wooden pallet with my nose pointing into the corner and felt my heart would break. I missed my home, and the twins, and my comfortable bed. I missed the good food and the big garden and the long walks. Why was I here?

In the weeks that followed each day was much the same as the one before. The aggressive dog in the kennel next door to me delivered four tiny squalling puppies one night. It was freezing cold and two were dead before morning. Our kennels were roughly scraped out and a fresh layer of fine sawdust dropped onto the concrete once a week. Sean, who usually did this, was sullen and slow. He smelled of tobacco and alcohol and gave off an aura of menace. He never paid us any attention except to shove us out of the way with his boot if we did not stay at the back of the kennel. He scraped up the bodies of the two dead puppies with his shovel and threw them into the wheel barrow. Our water bowls were never cleaned and we seldom had enough water to quench our thirst. The sawdust got into our eyes and between the pads on our feet and made us sore.

The fleas were thriving in our matted coats and we all scratched and bled and scratched some more. Some of us were losing our fur and had huge scaly bald patches that itched as well. It was misery, constant itching but so sore that when we scratched it made us whimper in pain.

The dog opposite who had been chewing her tail was one day carried out of her kennel and I never saw her again. Other dogs were sometimes carried off by Jock too, but they would be returned a short time later. I noticed that those dogs smelled differently when they returned, smells from the outside, like grass and leaves and earth.

I thought they had been for a walk and I dearly wished I could go too. One day I was carried outside. I was overwhelmed with joy and wriggled and wagged my tail in delight but Jock shook me by the scruff of my neck until my teeth rattled and cursed under his breath so I quickly fell limp in his arms, afraid to move.

I was taken to an outdoor kennel with high fencing where a male dog waited eagerly as I was dropped into his pen. The winter sunshine was dazzling but the fresh air was wonderful! I wanted to play with the male dog and we chased each other around until he tried to get on top of me. I squealed and tried to get free but Jock grabbed me and held me still. Suddenly I felt searing pain. My insides were on fire! I screamed and struggled but found I was locked together with the male dog and Jock was laughing and gripping my muzzle closed. After what seemed like forever the male dog released me and I was carried back to my kennel feeling bruised and terrified. A week later I endured the very same. It did not hurt as much but it was still frightening. I shivered and crouched in the back of my kennel for a long time afterwards.

A Little Dogs Prayer.   Author Jan McCulloch

Chapter Three

Some of the other dogs in the kennels near me began to have puppies. I smelled the strange scents of birth and heard the mewling cries of the new-borns. Sean brought plastic dog beds to put the mother and puppies in so that the puppies could not crawl under the pallet where their mothers could not reach them and die of hunger. But the plastic beds had no comfort and soon became soiled and foul smelling. I listened to the pitiful whimpering of the mother dogs when some or all of their puppies died. But despite the many deaths, there were a great many survivors. The puppies born into this place had a very hard time and I felt sad for them. I remembered my own puppyhood, full of warmth and tenderness and love. The big people who looked after my mother and siblings were kind and spoke softly. I remembered the gentle touch of their hands and remembered how happy my mother was. She loved her owners and they loved her. We puppies grew strong and confident and were clean and healthy. We looked forward to seeing the big people as much as our mother did. More than anything in this hell hole of a place my heart ached for a soft voice or a gentle touch.

Some weeks after being mated with the dog in the outside kennel I started to feel ravenously hungry. I never had enough to eat and while my puppies were growing inside me my ribs started to show. I was so thin and the cold seeped into my bones. Sometimes snow settled on the skylight windows. Our water froze. We shivered and suffered dreadfully through the long winter nights. The dog in the kennel next to me snuggled close to her surviving puppies to try keep them warm. None of us slept very well. Hunger gnawing at our insides. Sometimes some of the dogs snarled at each other through the bars of their kennels when food was thrown in. They became possessive of any morsel they could find. Some resorted to eating their own mess, such was their hunger. When food fell close to the bars between them they would leap upon it in a frenzy of flashing teeth. Jock or Sean would kick them away and the dogs would bite at their boots until they were kicked into submission or beaten with a stick.

One morning a stranger came to look at us. It was a woman who Jock and Sean called Maw. She walked past the kennels slowly, peering in at each of us in turn. We all crept away to the back of our kennels. We had learned through bitter experience to fear people in this place. None of us knew what to expect. She stopped at my kennel briefly, then moved on. After a few minutes we heard raised voices and the woman, Maw, was scooping large helpings of food into each kennel. She was angry and yelling at Sean, who usually fed us each day.

She did not say anything to any of us, no kind words or sympathy, but she made sure we had enough food at last. That night we at least had full tummies and felt better despite the cold.

It was a rainy day, we could hear the rain on the skylight windows and the water butt in the corner was filling slowly with a trickle from the hole in the roof. The puppies in the kennel next to me had started to eat food from the floor as well as suckling from their mother. Despite the awful conditions and the cold, they sometimes found the energy to play and I would watch them. It eased the monotony of the long days to see them play fight and roll around together. Their mother loved them dearly. She was very patient when they climbed on her and pulled her ears and she licked them to keep them as clean as she could.

 This morning, Sean brought a box into the building and set it down next to my kennel. He had the noose and pole with him. I heard the mother dog next door to me snarling. Her puppies scurried under her to hide, sensing her fear. Sean caught her in the noose and dragged her into a corner while he scooped up her puppies and dropped them into the box. Their mother was going wild on the end of the pole, but all her efforts were futile. He released her and slammed the door shut before she could escape. As Sean carried the puppies away she threw herself around the kennel, biting the bars in a frenzy until her mouth bled. I could feel her devastating grief for weeks afterwards. She seldom ate and lay in a corner whimpering under her breath. But when Sean came into the building her lips curled, exposing all her teeth, and her eyes glowed like coals. Her bitter hatred of him burned inside her. She shook with rage and drooled frothy saliva from her clenched jaws. It scared me to see how ferocious she looked and I would slink off into the corner furthest away from her and curl up in a tight ball. I too hated Jock and Sean. But I was afraid to growl or show them any anger. I had been brought up in a loving place where people were to be respected and where we learned manners. My instincts to defend myself had been dulled. I had a conflict inside me as I dearly wanted to fight back but all I could do was shiver in fear. I did not give Jock or Sean any cause to chastise me.

I saw other puppies being lifted away from their mothers. It seemed that as soon as they were starting to eat solid food they were taken away. The look in their mothers' eyes as they saw their children being carried away was harrowing. But they suffered in silence. Too afraid to shout for their babies. Some of the mothers gently whimpered in the night, a sound so filled with misery it made my heart ache.

A Little Dogs Prayer. Author Jan McCulloch

Chapter Four

My puppies were born during a storm. The rain was lashing against the sky light windows and thunder rumbled. I had severe pains in my abdomen and thought I was going to die, but when my first puppy arrived the pains eased for a while and I seemed to know just what to do. The instincts of my ancestors whispered to me to tell me to lick and clean this tiny life. He was a wriggling lively little pup who soon found his way to the warmth of my flank and his first feed. The next two puppies were girls and were just as lively. I licked them until they were dry and they were soon suckling next to their brother. My last puppy took a long time to be born. I had very strong pains for a long time and was getting anxious and unsettled. At last he was born, but he did not move. No matter how much I licked him, no matter how I nudged him with my nose, his tiny body was becoming cold. He was dead. The aggressive dog in the next kennel sat close to the bars and watched, softly whimpering. I felt comforted by her presence. She seemed to understand what I was going through. I could tell she was still mourning the loss of her own puppies and I was sad for her. I had the strongest feeling of love for my babies, I could not imagine the horror of having them taken away. The grief I felt for this one tiny puppy who had never drawn breath was bad enough, but having your children snatched away from you when you had fed and cleaned them, played with them and loved them for weeks must have been devastating.

I did not want Sean to see my puppies. When he came into the building I turned my back to the doorway hoping I could hide them from him, but my agitation startled them and they mewled and squeaked. He opened the door and stood towering above me. I was shaking in terror and my puppies felt my fear and went quiet. He used his boot to push my dead puppy away into the dirt. A whine escaped me, I did not want to lose this puppy even though he was dead, but the angry cussing from Sean silenced me and I watched in horror as he shovelled up my baby and threw him into the wheelbarrow with the dog mess. The aggressive dog in the kennel next door was growling deep in her throat and saliva was dripping from her jaws. Her eyes glowed red with hatred. Sean whacked the kennel door with his boot then moved on. Once he had gone, I settled down to keeping my puppies warm and clean. I cannot describe how wonderful it was to have these tiny bundles to love.

It did not seem to matter where I was anymore. These tiny lives were dependent on me and I was filled with maternal devotion. For the first time since I left my old home I was content. I loved the feel of those tiny squirming bodies snuggled into my flanks and soon learned the sounds of their voices and their scents so I could identify each one. The boy was a bossy little character who made sure he always had the best teat to feed from. One of the girls was a noisy little tyke who protested loudly when I was cleaning her. This worried me as I was afraid she would get me in trouble but she always fell silent when Jock or Sean came in. My fear was transmitted to her even at this early stage of her life. The other girl was a quiet and easily pleased pup. She reminded me of myself when I was tiny. She liked to crawl up under my chin once her tummy was full. I remembered that I had always liked to snuggle under my mother's chin too. But I remembered that my own mother never once showed any fear and we puppies were always warm and comfortable and clean. My puppies had already learned fear, experienced cold and were filthy.

And the hard plastic bed was far from comfortable. Sometimes I would dream that I was with my puppies in the cosy bed by the radiator at home. The twins were there, talking in whispers and Jade was feeding me delicious treats. I would wake up to feel the cold and smell the filth and I would whimper softly under my breath. I prayed that they would come and take me and my puppies away from this hell.

Sean paid little or no attention to me or my puppies in the first few weeks. I was left in peace to enjoy my time with them. The puppies opened their eyes and started to grow stronger on their legs. They were soon playing and rolling around together. When they climbed on me and pulled my ears I did not have the heart to chastise them. The aggressive dog in the kennel next door would lie close to the bars so that my puppies could pull her fur and even get her tail sometimes. She was comforted by their games because she missed her own puppies. We knew we were spoiling them by not teaching them any manners but we felt their lives were hard enough without further punishment from us. And somehow their antics relieved the boredom and frustration of being locked up. I was certainly far more tolerant than my own mother had been with me and my siblings. But when big boy pup bullied his sisters I admonished him as I was afraid their yelping might annoy Sean or Jock. I had seen a couple of puppies in other kennels being shaken violently by the scruff of their necks because they were noisy.

Although it was still cold, the nights were getting shorter and a weak sunlight filtered through the grubby sky light windows. My puppies had started to eat some of the dog food that was thrown onto the floor of the kennel. One morning Sean came in carrying a box. He set it down by my door. I was shivering with terror, shielding my puppies who were hiding behind me, squashed up to the wall in the corner. Sean had not brought the noose and pole this time. He knew I was not an aggressive dog. He shoved me aside and lifted my puppies from me and dropped them into the box. None of them made a sound. Shocked, I tried to follow him but he beat me back and slammed the door. He walked away without a backward glance leaving me alone, staring after him.

Never in my life had I felt such anguish. A guttural wail escaped my throat despite my fear of making a noise. I paced and circled the kennel in despair. The aggressive dog in the kennel next door put her nose through the bars and whimpered but I could not be consoled. My babies were gone.

A Little Dogs Prayer. Author Jan McCulloch

Chapter Five

When the twins ran out of school and made their way to the gates they saw mummy was waiting there instead of sitting in the car as she usually did. She was not smiling. She looked like she had been crying. The twins slowed to a walk as they approached her. She kneeled in front of them and told them that she had something very sad to tell them but they both had to be brave. She told them that Bonny was gone. They both wailed as they got into the car, hugging each other while their little shoulders shook with sobs. Jade saw that the dog crate was no longer in the back of the car and wailed even more.

When they got home, mummy sat them at the kitchen table and spoke to them in a very serious way, almost as if they were grown-ups and not eight years old. She explained that mummy and daddy were getting a divorce and that daddy had gone to live in another place and mummy and the twins were going to live in a smaller house where no dogs were allowed. The twins could not believe what they were hearing. They asked lots of questions about Bonny but mummy told them firmly that Bonny had gone to a new family where she would be looked after and that the twins had to forget about her. There were going to be far more important things to worry about.

That night, in their beds, the twins sobbed themselves to sleep. They wanted daddy to go bring Bonny back and they wanted to stay in this house with mummy and daddy and Bonny just like before.

In the morning, there was no Bonny to wake them up. Mummy came into the bedroom and opened the curtains. Both twins had dark circles around their eyes and mummy started to cry as she held the two of them close for a moment before sending them away to get washed and dressed. The twins felt as though their little hearts were breaking. Mummy told them that daddy was coming to see them at the weekend and would take them to his new place. Neither of them wanted to know about daddy or his new place. They just wanted Bonny.

In the garden, a squirrel was stealing nuts from the bird feeder and burying them in the autumn leaves.

The journey to school was a quiet one. None of the usual chatter. Mummy was quiet too. The twins could tell she was very upset. They kissed and hugged her as they climbed out of the car and then held hands as they went into school.

Miss Holden took the register and then had a look at her class of eight year olds. The twins, Ellie and Jade Dalton were not their usual chirpy selves. They looked ashen and subdued.

Miss Holden set tasks for everyone and then went to sit with the twins who were taking out their reading books along with the rest of the class. Jade looked on the verge of tears and Ellie was holding her hand under the table. Miss Holden asked them if everything was okay but her gentle sympathetic voice was just too much and they both started to cry.

The rest of the class craned around in their seats to see what was happening so Miss Holden told them all to sit quietly and read while she took the twins out of the classroom to speak to them in private. She sat them in the cloakroom and gave them both tissues to dry their eyes. It was Ellie who spoke first, she told Miss Holden that they were missing their pet dog Bonny because she had gone to a new home.

Miss Holden was very kind and said that she used to have a dog who she had to part with so she understood how sad it could be. She took them back into class and was quietly relieved that the problem with the twins was not serious.

At lunchtime, the twins ate nothing. They sat in the school canteen avoiding contact with the other children, just sitting sniffling into the tissues Miss Holden had given them. They didn't speak to anyone, not even each other.

When the bell rang for home time Miss Holden walked with the girls out to the school gates. Jade and Ellie went straight to their mother and burst into tears. She hugged them and looked at Miss Holden, her eyes full of anguish, her face pale. She sent the twins to get in the car and then had a brief conversation with their teacher, telling her that there was more to it than just the dog. The twins father had left them and they were all devastated. Miss Holden was sympathetic and suggested the twins might have a day off school the next day. The twins had clearly taken it all very badly.

Jade and Ellie were sitting in the car still holding hands when mummy came back from talking to their teacher. Mummy tried to be cheerful and suggested a trip to McDonalds for tea, but both girls shook their heads and did not speak.

At home, the twins went to their room while mummy brought the washing in from the line. They usually helped with small jobs like these but today they did not feel like doing anything. In their bedroom, they lay on their beds and sobbed into their pillows.

Mummy called them down for tea but they pushed the food around their plates and could not eat. She tried to talk to them about daddy and about the new place they were going to live but her words died on her lips as they looked at her with so much sorrow, tears trickling down their faces. She ran a warm bath for them and afterwards gave them hot chocolate and settled them into their beds. Her own heart was breaking. Her husband had left her for another woman. Someone he met at work. She was still reeling from the shock. The betrayal was bitter bile in her throat and her whole body trembled. Tears flooded her cheeks as she thought of how upset the twins were.

Why did he have to put them all through this? She knew deep down that her marriage had been a sham. She knew that Brian had not been happy for a long time. The extended periods of sullen silences and the harsh looks. Working late at the office. He had not held her in his arms for years. And she hadn't wanted him to. But the betrayal still hurt.

A Little Dogs Prayer. Author Jan McCulloch

Chapter Six

Brian had not been happy in his marriage for a long time. Just going through the motions. He could remember happy times of course, but they seemed so far away. And if he was honest with himself those times were before the twins came along. They had taken all of Jeans attention. He felt like an invisible man most of the time. So when Lucy in the office started giving him attention he felt alive again and jumped into a full blown affair. He and Lucy laughed a lot. They talked a lot too, about hopes and dreams. The future. His marriage was dead to him long before he made the decision to leave.

Parting with the dog had tweaked his conscience. He had not told his wife how much he had been paid for Bonny. He had pocketed all the money himself. He answered an advert he had seen online, someone who lived on a farm wanted a pet. They offered good money, and a farm home sounded perfect. One phone call was all it took. He met the new owner in a car park one afternoon, was paid handsomely and away the dog went. One less responsibility to worry about. The dog would have great fun on a farm. What dog wouldn't?

The new flat that he and Lucy had rented was a dream come true. Clean polished floors, huge windows that let in lots of light and magnificent views onto the rooftops of the city. One bedroomed of course. No way was there going to be any sleepovers for the twins. Visits maybe. But Brian did not intend to spend more time than was necessary with them. He and Lucy had plans that did not include children. Their aim was to move abroad. Lucy had recently inherited a lump sum from an aged relative, along with some property in France. Brian thanked his lucky stars that he and Lucy had found each other. No more rat race, struggling to pay bills and never ending financial worry. He knew that the sale of his marital home would provide sufficient funds for Jean and the twins. He was not a complete cad. He would see them right and then in just a few months he would be gone. Fatherhood had never suited him. He had been uncomfortable with the twins since they were born. Hated all the sleepless nights, the nappies, and most especially the way Jean always put them first. And she was always too tired for anything he wanted to do. But add to that the weight she had gained and how she seldom took care of her appearance anymore, it was hardly any wonder her appeal had waned. Lucy though. She was a real woman who knew how to look after a man. She always smelled fresh, dressed well and gave him her full attention.

When his wife Jean phoned him to tell him the twins were devastated, he was initially conceited enough to think they were upset that he had left. He felt qualms about having to face them at the weekend. He could almost picture their tearful faces and was not keen on having to explain that he and their mother were getting a divorce. No doubt Jean will have laid the blame firmly at his door.

However, when Jean told him that the twins did not want to see him because he had got rid of the dog, he spewed forth a verbal tirade of abuse, accusing her of trying to make him look like the bad guy when in fact he had suffered years of misery with her always giving him grief. He did not let her try to explain, and when she tried to ask him where Bonny had gone and could he please try get her back, he discharged all the pent-up frustration of nine years of misery and slammed the phone down.

Moments later he laughed out loud. Getting rid of the dog had freed him from having to see the twins at all! And as for getting the dog back, he had no address for the new owner and had not bothered to keep their number. And even if he could contact them, he was not about to do so …. He had a tidy sum of money from the sale of the dog that he planned to use to buy Lucy something special. A romantic candlelit meal at a select restaurant and a fancy piece of jewellery. He smiled at his thoughtfulness. That would make Lucy happy.

A Little Dogs Prayer. Author Jan McCulloch

Chapter Seven

Jean was seething when Brian hung up on her. She tried to redial but no reply. The twins had listened to her side of the conversation, heard her trying to find out where Bonny was. They saw how distressed she was after the call and they came and hugged her. Ellie did not cry but Jade shook with sobs. Jean gently pushed them away after a tight squeeze and told them they would have to be brave. Ellie nodded solemnly but Jade ran upstairs to throw herself onto her bed weeping inconsolably. When Ellie went to her and laid a hand on her shoulder, Jade shook her off. Ellie sighed and went back downstairs.

In the weeks that followed things did not improve for Jade. Her eyes were constantly bloodshot, she was looking thin and frail and had no interest in food. Despite Jean and Ellie's best efforts, Jade slipped further and further into herself. Her school work suffered but most importantly, her relationship with her twin suffered. Ellie was starting to lose patience with Jade. She wanted her sister to be fun again, to play games and do things together. But Jade ignored her sisters' pleas and instead she relentlessly searched the internet looking at pictures of dogs in the dog pound and dog rescue shelters. She felt sure she would see Bonny there one day. Felt sure that Bonny would have run away from where ever she was and would be trying to get home.

Jean could not bear to see how the loss of Bonny was affecting Jade. She sat with her one day to write an advert to put on Facebook. It was a photo of Bonny and a request for anyone who knew her whereabouts to get in touch. Sadly, although very many people thought they had seen the little dog in the photo, none turned out to be Bonny.

Jade was not sleeping. She was obsessed with searching the internet. Jean had to give her a curfew of no internet access after nine o'clock at night. That was when Jade started self-harming. She sat on the bathroom floor and cut long welts into her arms. Ellie saw the jagged wounds and told mummy.

Jean sobbed and held Jade in her arms. But Jade did not weep. She sat there limply, staring into space. Jean made an appointment for Jade to see the Doctor. She was not sure if this was just because of the dog or because their father had made no contact. Additionally, they were moving to a smaller house in the coming week. Maybe it was all too much for her and Jade needed professional help to deal with her issues.

Ellie helped to pack things in the boxes that Jean brought from the supermarket. Jade just lay on her bed and stared at the ceiling.

 Even her manic searching of the internet had ceased. Jean had tried sympathy, had tried cajoling, and had eventually broken down in tears of frustration. Ellie sobbed with her mum, then shouted at Jade through her tears, saying Bonny was her dog too and didn't she think anyone else missed her? But Jade just closed her eyes and turned away.

The Doctor spoke softly to Jade and asked her some questions but Jade did not reply. Jean tried to speak for her but the Doctor held up her hand and shook her head. She wanted to see if any of her questions would get a reaction from the small pale child in front of her.

The child's twin was sitting quietly next to her mother, anxious and wide eyed, but otherwise looking robust and healthy with colour in her cheeks.

After a short time, the Doctor advised that a child psychologist might be the answer, and made a call directly from her desk. Jean was overwhelmed with relief. She just wanted Jade to be her old self again and felt that a child psychologist might be able to get through to Jade where she herself had failed.

An appointment was made for Jade to visit a Doctor Saunders the very next day at a local clinic. As they were leaving the surgery the Doctor handed Jean some leaflets about mental health disorders and domestic violence helplines. Jean had a lump in her throat as she walked the twins back to the car. Mental Health? So Jade was suffering from a mental illness. She felt her insides tighten and her jaw lock as she thought of Brian and what he had done to their family. Jade had been a perfectly normal, happy youngster just a couple of months ago, yet here she was, about to be seen by a psychologist! As for domestic violence, Jean felt that she herself would be the one dishing out the violence if she could only get her hands on Brian!

That night Jean tried to talk to Jade about the appointment the next day, but Jade did not respond. She snuggled close to Jean on the sofa and let Jean stroke her hair. But she did not talk. Ellie was starting to feel jealous of all the attention Jade was getting so she snuggled up to Jean too. The three of them sat there like that for several hours until Jean roused the twins and sent them to bed. She was feeling emotionally drained and despite long talks with friends on the phone she felt so very alone. She was not looking forward to having to tell her mother about the psychologist. Jeans mother was a hard, bitter woman who would no doubt have plenty to say about it all. Her favourite quote was 'Spare the rod, spoil the child!' so there would be no empathy or compassion from that quarter.

When the twins were asleep, Jean sat in the darkness and thought about the events that had brought her to where she was now. She thought back to when the twins were born and how happy she had been. And she thought about Brian. Had he ever been happy? Had he ever seemed proud of his children? She really could not remember him ever even holding them of his own volition. He held them when they were handed to him, and later, he held them when they climbed on his knee. But she could not remember him ever looking upon them with affection. She shook her head. She had made up for his lack of interest by telling the girls how proud their daddy was of them, by telling them how much their daddy loved them. She had filled in all the gaping holes of his indifference. But she did not think she had fooled the girls for a second. Ellie was not in the least interested in her father or what he was doing, and Jade positively hated him. Neither of them wanted to see him or speak to him. As she turned out the lights and went up to bed she wished she had not let Brian take Bonny away. But at the time, she had been so overwhelmed and shocked by him saying he was leaving that she had not argued. She had thought that at least the little dog would have a happy life on a farm. She could never have imagined in her wildest nightmares that Jade would end up as a psychiatric outpatient due to missing the dog.

The appointment with the psychologist was just before lunch. Ellie had gone into to school, reluctantly, on her own. Jean told her she was not ill so did not get time off school. Ellie was resentful and sullen because she felt left out. Jean had sighed and bitten back words of anger. The strain was getting to them all. Instead she promised Ellie a nice treat at the weekend for being so brave and sensible.

The psychologists room had lots of toys and bright colours and pictures. Jade did not acknowledge the Doctor when spoken to. When Jean showed Dr Saunders the fierce gashes on her daughters arms a silent tear rolled down her cheek.

Doctor Saunders asked Jean lots of questions. Then he asked if he might speak to her in private. Jade had not showed any interest in any of her surroundings and was sitting slumped in a chair looking deathly pale. The Doctor took Jean into the next room where she saw that there was a two-way mirror on the wall. She and the Doctor sat and had a coffee while the Doctor explained that the purpose of leaving Jade alone for a little while was to see if she took an interest in anything in the adults' absence.

After half an hour Jade had not moved a fraction. Dr Saunders touched Jeans arm and told her that Jade needed to be admitted to a Psychiatric childrens ward for further evaluation. Jean broke down in tears.

When Dr Saunders explained to Jade that she was going into hospital for a little while, Jade did not react. Jean took her hand and led her out into the corridor while the Doctor booked her a bed in a ward at the local Hospital.

It was all Jean could do not to sob and hug Jade. But she knew she had to be strong so she waited for the Doctor to bring her the directions to the ward at the Hospital where Jade was to be admitted, then walked her out to the car.

The Hospital was bright and pleasant, and the staff were very friendly. Jean stayed until Jade was settled into a bed on a mixed children's ward. There were children of various ages, some lively and some lying motionless on their beds just as Jade was. Her heart went out to them. As she was leaving she looked back into the ward to wave to Jade, but her daughters eyes were closed. She looked so weak and frail. Jean stifled a sob as she pushed through the swing doors out into the corridor. With tears in her eyes she returned home to an empty house where she threw herself down on the sofa and sobbed into the cushions.

A Little Dogs Prayer. Author Jan McCulloch

Chapter Eight

The mobile phone rang and echoed through the rambling old stone farmhouse. Morag Allan roused her ample frame from her armchair in front of the roaring fire where she had been toasting her toes. It took her a moment to establish which of the half dozen mobile phones was actually ringing, each phone labelled with the name of a dog breed written on it in an untidy scrawl. Poodle, King Charles, West Highland Terrier, Maltese, Schnauzer and Bichon. Ah yes, this one was for the fluffy white poodle puppies she had advertised only this morning in the local paper. Soon she was relating her rehearsed speech to the caller about the wonderful pedigree puppies she had for sale. She smiled smugly as she ended the call and then went to pour herself another beer. She threw a couple of logs on the fire and relaxed into her chair again. The wind was whistling around the buildings and somewhere outside a branch tapped against a window pane. She would relax for a few more minutes then go finish preparing dinner for her boys. Roast beef and all the trimmings. It had been a good year, over seventy pups sold so far and all at very good prices.

The boys came in just as it was getting dark. The eldest, Jock, had fiery red hair and was built like a bear. He had a huge appetite but it was nothing compared to that of his younger brother Sean, who ate like a horse. The two of them piled their plates high and sat down at the scrubbed pine kitchen table. The warmth from the stove brought bright red spots to their cheeks and droplets of sweat appeared on their brows.

Morag let them eat a while before telling them that she needed a litter of pups in for a bath as she had customers coming in the morning. The eldest, Jock, nodded as he stuffed a whole Yorkshire pudding into his almost toothless mouth. He had lost his teeth in bare fist fights over the years and sported a pair of cauliflower ears and a flattened nose. Breathing through his mouth was a necessity so he gulped down his food and gasped for air between mouthfuls. His brother Sean took a swig of beer from a can and wiped his mouth on the back of his sleeve. He did not have the war wounded features of his older brother. His face was oval and smooth. He grunted and swallowed a great piece of beef. He shuffled in his seat and broke wind and his mother whacked him around the head with a tea towel. He sniggered and did it again.

After the meal, Morag filled the big Belfast sink with warm water and urged Sean to bring in the litter of Poodle pups. He shrugged into a heavy coat, slid on his boots and slouched out of the kitchen, taking a box and a torch out of the hallway as he went. He returned minutes later with three tiny filthy puppies cowering in the bottom of the box.

Morag lifted them out one by one and dropped them into the water, scrubbing them vigorously with washing up liquid until their white coats shone. After briefly towelling them dry she dropped them into a cat basket with a soft clean blanket and set them down by the side of the table.

None of them uttered a sound. They had been lifted from the warmth of their mothers flank in the darkness by the big people that their mother feared so much and had been shocked to the core by the bath and the rough handling. Morag did not say a single word throughout the procedure and handled them with no compassion.

The job was to get them clean, which she did, and then she returned to the cosy fireside and her bottle of beer. Her favourite programme was on television so she never gave them another thought. The three pups huddled together, chilled by the bath and afraid of the strange noises and smells.

It was a very long night for them and twice they whimpered softly, but first Jock kicked the cat box to terrify them into silence, then Sean did the same. They did not make another sound.

In the morning, Morag shoved a bowl of soaked dog food in front of them. They timidly licked the moisture from it as they craved a drink but they did not eat despite their hunger. Morag was not worried about this as she did not want them getting the runs or being sick before her customers came.

The first family to visit that day had three rowdy children and had never had a dog before but thought it would be nice for the kids to have something to play with. Morag took their money and told them she was thrilled that the pup was going to such a lovely home. The father mumbled something about being told they should see the puppies with their mother, so Morag told them a tale about the mother dog being at the vets to be spayed as she did not want any more puppies. The father nodded sagely and a pup was thrust into the arms of the eldest child while the other two screeched and fought and demanded a turn at holding him. The family left with lots of smiles and goodwill and Morag stuffed the eight hundred pounds into the big blue vase on the sideboard.

The second customer was an old friend who was after a couple of pups for a client of his. Morag had a network of dog dealing buddies who regularly called by to swap dogs or to buy worming tablets. Morag told them she bought the wormers in bulk on the internet and she could get them cheap. The worming tablets were in fact from a greyhound racing kennel where Sean's pal worked. He got them for the price of a few beers down the local. Morag had instructed Sean to worm the dogs in the buildings but he flushed the tablets down the toilet because he could not be bothered grabbing fifty or more dogs to push a tablet down each of their throats. Especially when some of them would have your hand off as soon as look at you.

Once the last two pups had been bundled into a box and dropped into the back of the van, Morag's friend settled down for a nice lunch of roast beef sandwiches washed down with lager shandy. They both lamented the days of old when you could have a good beer swilling session without fear of being caught drink driving. Morag and her friend Jimmy tucked in to apple pie and custard after the roast beef and then Jimmy said his farewells. There was a good four-hour drive ahead of him and a ride on the ferry. He would not be home before dark. He shoved a wad of cash into Morags hands as he left. As soon as the door closed she counted it quickly and dropped twelve hundred pounds into the big blue vase on the sideboard. Not as much as she got for the first pup, but then Jimmy needed to make a pound or two from the sale. Pleased with her mornings work, she threw a log on the fire and settled down for an afternoon snooze.

Jock and Sean had fed and watered the dogs. Sean did the bitches and young stock while Jock did the stud dogs. It generally took them a couple of hours between them. Then they went off to the pub in the village to watch the footy. It being Saturday they would have a lie in tomorrow. Neither of them worked on a Sunday. They both had plenty of cash in their pockets. Maw paid them well.

A Little Dogs Prayer. Author Jan McCulloch

Chapter Nine

Dr Saunders finished writing up his notes about Jade Dalton. He sighed and took off his glasses. Pinching the bridge of his nose momentarily, he leaned back in his chair. After some weeks of daily sessions with Jade he did not feel that he had made any headway at all. She was not uncooperative, she followed instructions such as getting a shower, making her bed, going for a walk in the Hospital grounds. But she simply did not talk. She would speak sometimes, occasional words of greeting, or please and thank you, but she would not really *talk.* She clammed up as soon as any personal questions were directed at her. In exasperation during the last session that day, Dr Saunders had spread his hands and asked Jade if there was anything at all that she cared about. She visibly flinched. He saw it. Like she had been spiked with a pin. But no sooner had he seen it, her facial muscles relaxed and it was gone. But there was something there. *Something.*

In discussions with the girls' mother, Dr Saunders had established that the father had left. He tentatively asked if there could have been sexual abuse. Mrs Dalton recoiled in horror before exclaiming vehemently absolutely not! For one thing, her husband was seldom at home and for another he had never actually *liked* the girls. This statement pointed Dr Saunders down the route of the child possibly blaming herself for the departure of her father. When he mentioned her father however, Jade did not react at all. He asked her if she was upset about moving to a smaller house? No reaction. Dr Saunders decided to prescribe some mild antidepressants for Jade to try help her relax enough to start talking.

Jade took her tablets without a fuss. They helped her go to sleep but she awoke in the night screaming from nightmares. Dr Saunders and the nurses asked her what the nightmares were about but Jade did not seem to remember. Or if she did, she would not discuss them. Dr Saunders decided to increase the dose a little. Jade then slept soundly through the night, but was groggy and bewildered during the day, often falling asleep in the afternoons. Despite being sedated, Jade was no more relaxed than she had been before. If anything, she was less inclined to talk at all. But Dr Saunders maintained the dose of drugs while he wracked his brains and looked up case studies, even phoning colleagues to ask their opinions. One bonus was that Jade had ceased self-harming. That, at least, gave him something positive to tell her mother.

Jade lay on her bed staring at the ceiling. She felt light headed and woozy. Jade vaguely understood that the Doctor and nurses and her mother were all trying to help her. But in her head, she had built a special little world that only she and Bonny shared. She could smell Bonny, feel her, hear her. Bonny was right there in her head and she was never going to leave her. She smiled as she drifted in and out of sleep.

When she first started on the tablets, they made it hard to see Bonny and Jade would wake up in a panic, thrashing around in the bed, feeling like she was wading through mud to try to get to the little dog.

But after a few days and a higher dose, Jade slept soundly. The nightmares were gone.

Early one morning when Liz the cleaner came into the ward to empty the bins and dust the bedside cabinets, she saw Jade stroking her pillow and whispering. She looked like she was talking in her sleep. Moving closer Liz paused at the end of the bed to listen. She could hear Jade quite clearly, and the girl seemed to be talking to a dog. She was stroking her pillow and telling it that they were going to go for a walk, and they were going to find the special ball.

Liz was a dog lover. She had a small chubby mongrel of her own called Rupert, or Roo for short, who she thought the world of. Her heart went out to this little girl. She did not understand anything about mental breakdowns or mental health problems, but she fully understood what it felt like to love a dog. Liz walked away softly, deep in thought. She had an idea.

The next morning Liz did her rounds of the wards as usual and then went to find Jade. The girl was sitting on her bed staring into space. Liz pulled up a chair and sat beside her. Jade did not seem to realise she had company so Liz leant forward and touched her arm. Jade was startled and jumped violently, making Liz gasp and draw away sharply. Jade stared at her, looking confused and anxious, so Liz smiled and took some pictures out of her pocket, offering them to Jade to look at. The photos were of a small fat dog. A much-loved dog, wearing a little jacket in some of the photos, and holding toys in another. The bright eyes and cheeky face of this little dog, with his shaggy eyebrows and his pricked-up ears made a massive impact on Jade. Liz was overwhelmed by the series of emotions that flashed over Jades face in that moment. The girls heart was clearly broken. She clutched the photos, her eyes brimming with tears, her lips trembling, before looking at Liz beseechingly. In that moment, it seemed to Jade that this lady knew exactly how she felt. She threw herself off the bed and into Liz's lap, wrapping her arms around her neck, her shoulders shaking with heart-rending sobs. Liz held her close and let her weep. One of the nurses saw what was happening and ran for Doctor Saunders. This looked like a break through!

When the doctor came into the ward he saw Jade wrapped in the arms of the cleaning lady. The girl had stopped sobbing and was sitting quietly on Liz's lap, shuffling through some photos. He took a few tentative steps forward and asked if he might see them. Jade looked up at him and he saw in her eyes something that he had not seen before. Hope. He took the photos from her and flicked through them, surprised to note that all the photos were very much the same. A small dog, a terrier of some kind sleeping in a dog basket. Doctor Saunders could not imagine why those photos had sparked a reaction in Jade. He was not fond of dogs. In fact, he was not keen on animals at all. They had their uses of course. Laboratory animals were particularly useful. So after a brief glance at the photos he handed them back to Jade and asked if he might see Liz in his office for a moment.

Liz was so pleased that the little girl had shown such delight in the photos of Roo. When she looked back as she left the ward she could see Jade smiling while she spread the photos out in front of her on the bed. Doctor Saunders asked Liz to take a seat and closed his office door. His office was large and furnished with heavy antique drawers, a book case and a very large oak desk. There was a filing cabinet in the corner with a large pot plant on it, and the walls were adorned with certificates of achievement in the field of Psychology, all in gold frames. It was unbearably warm, Liz thought. The air felt thick as syrup.

Liz was smiling up at him expectantly, but her smile faltered when she saw the Doctor looking stonily down on her. He looked away briefly and paced up and down in front of his desk, then proceeded to give Liz a harsh admonishment for bringing the photos into the hospital and for giving them to Jade.

He told Liz in no uncertain terms that she had acted in a most irresponsible manner and that he was giving her a formal verbal warning about her conduct. Liz stammered a few words of protest but was silenced when Doctor Saunders growled that the reaction to those photos, although seemingly favourable, could have deep seated repercussions for Jade. Indeed, Liz should think herself lucky that there had in fact been a favourable reaction because things could have been altogether unfavourable and may have caused Jade irreparable mental damage! He then told Liz that he was going to have her rota on the Wards changed to exclude her from all the Children's Medical Areas. She would continue her work within the Hospital, but only on the Adult Wards and only if he had her assurances that she would simply get on with her work and not interfere in professional areas of expertise that she knew nothing about.

Liz left the Doctors office with her head down. Her cheeks were burning with humiliation and she made straight for the exit without returning to the ward to retrieve her photos. By the time she arrived home she had calmed herself but she still trembled a little as she put the key in the front door. Roo was there to greet her, wagging his tail so hard that his whole body wriggled. She knelt and hugged him briefly before going through to the kitchen to put the kettle on. Roo had his own doggie flap in the door that led out into the back garden from the kitchen so he could go in and out whenever he pleased. He sat at her feet looking up at her expectantly, anticipating the biscuit that he might share once the tea had been made.

Liz had always been a very sensitive person. When she was a child she had been able to see spirits and could hear their whispers sometimes to this day. She wished she had retained her psychic abilities into adulthood but somehow as the years had passed her spirit friends had almost faded away. She was, however, an empath. She could feel other people's emotions so strongly sometimes that it was hard to know if those emotions were theirs or her own.

She had felt an overwhelming grief coming from the small child at the Hospital. It had reminded her of when she was a child and her very first pet, a cat called Twiggy, had died. She remembered how acutely she'd felt the little cats' loss, and how none of her friends or relatives had even the slightest inclination of how devastated she was about losing him. Liz shook her head sadly at the recollection, but then she smiled. She was remembering how that little cat visited her in spirit to console her. She could still hear his soft purring and feel the weight of him in her lap if she sat quietly and thought about him. But Liz did not think that Jade was suffering a bereavement. There was more to it than that. Despite Doctor Saunders verbal warning to keep away from the children's wards, Liz was already hatching a plan. She believed that Jade needed more than drugs and fancy psychotherapy! Somehow, Liz was going to help that little girl. She went into her cosy sitting room to light the log burner, then took her tarot cards from their place on the mantelpiece. It had been a long time since she had felt the urge to consult the cards, so she held them close to her heart and closed her eyes to empty her mind and focus exclusively on the task ahead. Roo came in and settled at her feet and was soon dozing in the warmth of the fire.

Only the crack and hiss of wood sizzling in the burner disturbed the silence. Outside, a squall of rain spattered the window. Liz felt herself relaxing and gently started to shuffle the cards.

A Little Dogs Prayer. Author Jan McCulloch

Chapter Ten

Doctor Saunders phoned Jean Dawson to ask her to come in to his office for a chat. He had been mulling over recent events concerning Jades reaction to the photos that Liz the cleaning lady had given her. He was resentful that all his own efforts had resulted in no clear improvement in Jades condition, but he was not about to admit anything of the sort to Jades mother. He had decided to proffer a theory that his prescription drugs had settled Jades mind to such a degree that she had ceased self-harming and started to open up to therapy. He decided to suggest that Jade return home and become an outpatient to the psychiatric clinic once a week.

When Jean was sitting in his office, Doctor Saunders told her that he was relying on both she and Jades sister, Ellie, to make notes about Jades behaviour at home but to do so discretely. He did not want Jade to know that she was being observed. But he wanted an insight into how she was coping with returning to family life. This information would be useful he said, in his weekly therapy clinic with Jade.

Jean was grateful to Doctor Saunders. But as she left his office and went to tell Jade that she was coming home at last, she felt a prickle of apprehension. She was worried how Jade would cope at home. Ellie had developed new friendships at school, enjoyed having sleepovers and seemed quite popular with several of the girls in her class. She had put a lot of effort into her bedroom at the new house, clearly establishing it as her very own. It had been difficult when they had first moved house as Ellie seemed to be driven by a desire to wipe out any trace of Jade. She threw out some of her twins' belongings and Jean had to rescue them from the dustbin. Ellie was sullen and uncommunicative when it came to anything to do with Jade. She had stopped visiting at the hospital weeks ago, preferring to spend time with her friends. Jean had tried to talk to Ellie about it but Ellie complained that the hospital was boring and Jade never even spoke so why bother going there? It was with dismay one day that Jean overheard Ellie and her friends discussing Jade. They were giggling and describing her as a fruit loop. Jean felt she had to say something to the girls, but when she did, Ellie glared at her and later told her that Jean had humiliated her in front of her friends. Jean angrily sent Ellie to her room after telling her that mental illness was not to be ridiculed. Later that evening Jean, sitting alone in the kitchen, wondered if her daughters would ever regain the happy relationship they used to share. It appeared Ellie was ashamed of Jade. Young children could be very cruel and any hint of something they did not fully understand could trigger unpleasantness and bullying.

Ellie, for the first time in her life, was glowing under a spotlight of attention both at home and at school. She loved having a room to herself and her mother's full attention and enjoyed her new-found popularity at school. At first the girls in her class had made fun of her about having a sister in the looney bin.

Ellie had saved herself from further ridicule by acting out as if she herself was not quite right in the head either, until the other children collapsed in fits of laughter and decided that Ellie was in fact good fun to be around.

Ellie was treated with sympathy and kindness by her teacher and by the parents of her new friends. They believed her to be an innocent victim of a particularly unpleasant divorce compounded by suffering the trauma of having a mentally ill twin. Ellie thrived on the attention and pushed Jade further and further from her mind. She had resented the attention that Jade had been getting so once Jade had been hospitalised Ellie silently prayed that her mad sister would never come back.

When Jean walked into the children's ward she saw Jade sitting with a smaller child in her lap. They were looking at a book together and Jean felt a lump rise in her throat. Jade looked across and smiled. Jean blinked away the tears. Despite Jade being thin and pale, there was a spark in her eyes that had been absent for a long time. Bending down, Jean whispered that Jade could get her things together and come home. Anxiety flashed across Jades face but she nodded and set the smaller child down, handing her the book they had been looking at, before turning to hug her mum tightly.

In the car on the way home Jean explained that the new house was smaller than the old one but closer to the school. She told Jade that they would walk down to meet Ellie at home time.

Once they arrived home Jade wandered around the new house to get her bearings while Jean made toast and jam for them both. Jade had started to shiver. The hospital ward had been a great deal warmer than the house so Jean brought her a warm fleecy throw to wrap around her shoulders. Jade sat at the kitchen table and stroked the fleece absently while she ate her toast. Jean watched her carefully. There did not seem to be any signs of withdrawal and Jade looked across at her mum and smiled briefly.

Jade was feeling a mixture of agitation and fear. The new house felt alien to her, as did her mother, despite how kind and affectionate she was trying to be. Jade could sense the undercurrents of her mother's emotions and they were not comparing favourably with how calm she appeared on the surface. Since the day the nice cleaning lady had given her the photos of the little dog, Jade had been developing a heightened sense of awareness regarding the emotions of anyone nearby. At first Jade thought it was a little frightening to be bombarded with emotions that seemed to be her own but once she realised that she was picking up on other people's thoughts she learned to control them and keep them apart from her own. She was also experiencing a wonderful feeling of calm and love that came into her head with the soft voice of her friend the cleaning lady Liz. Jade could not explain how her friend spoke to her like that. Maybe she, Jade, was hallucinating. She was, after all, in a psychiatric ward. She had heard one of the other patients talking about hearing voices so maybe that was happening to her too. But she told no one. The soft voice was reassuring and brought with it a sense of calm and wellbeing. Jade had tried to talk back to her friend in her head but found herself feeling dizzy so she just listened and smiled and hoped that Liz would understand.

She was apprehensive about her mother's agitation and fear but did not broach the subject. Instead, she dutifully finished her toast and got ready to walk to school to collect Ellie. It had not escaped her notice that Ellie had discarded all of Jades belongings, clothes, toys and books into a small box room next to their mother's bedroom. Jade had picked up a sensory prickle of exclusion. She was not looking forward to seeing her twin. Not now that she knew Ellie would not be at all pleased to see her.

A Little Dog's Prayer. Author Jan McCulloch

Chapter Eleven.

Practicing telepathy was proving very tiring and Liz found herself snoozing in front of her log burner most evenings. She had been astonished at her first experience of communicating with Jade through the little girls thought channels. Liz had wondered if she was dreaming or if she was going mad, but since the day she had returned to the Tarot she had gratefully opened up a fresh contact with her spirit friends and was being guided by them. Liz understood that Jade was listening and trying to respond. And it was good to feel how calm and comforted the little girl was.

Earlier in the evening the spirits had shown Liz vivid pictures of a farmhouse kitchen occupied by a large woman who was cooking on a wonderfully shiny aga stove. Two young men were sitting at a giant scrubbed pine table, playing cards and drinking beer. When the image was firmly in her minds eye, Liz could feel a skin crawling sensation of filth. There was a smell too, a stench unlike anything she had ever smelled before. This puzzled Liz because the scene before her was one of warm, clean domesticity but her senses were telling her otherwise. She reached for her notebook and jotted down what she had seen and how she had experienced the filth and stench. None of it made sense now. But her spirit friends whispered their approval.

After making herself a cup of tea and placing a handful of biscuits on a small plate Liz returned to her cosy sitting room where Roo was waiting in eager anticipation. He knew he would share the biscuits. It was a nightly ritual that he greatly approved of. His little tail wagged and his eyes shone. But just as Liz passed him a biscuit, she became acutely aware of the foul smell she had experienced during her visitation from the spirits. Roo looked across the room, ignoring the proffered biscuit, and whined softly. Creeping to the back of the sofa, never taking his eyes from the spot across the room, he trembled. Liz could not see anything but the smell was almost unbearable. She sat down slowly and tried to empty her mind of thoughts. Someone or something was here trying to make contact. She closed her eyes for a few moments. When she opened them she was shocked to see a small skinny dog with matted fur, covered in excrement, cowering on the floor in front of her. The poor dog was covered in weeping sores and had lost an eye. It whimpered and gave a faint wag of its tail, but before Liz could reach down to comfort the poor little thing, it was gone.

Roo quickly recovered from his fright and rested his paw on Liz's arm to remind her about the biscuit. Liz was shaking her head and trying to understand what she had just seen and how it was connected to the image of the farmhouse kitchen. That smell was the same as the one earlier. Her spirit friends did not explain the presence of the dog. It was confusing because she knew she had seen it. She knew by how Roo had reacted that he had seen it too. She reached for her notebook and made a detailed entry, writing a description of the little dog and how it had behaved, what colour collar it was wearing, as well as the time and date.

Before she went to sleep that night, Liz sent telepathic comfort to Jade. When she tuned into Jades thought channels she was most disturbed by what she felt there. Poor Jade had clearly suffered some sort of emotional upheaval and was desperately grateful to feel Liz's presence. Liz soothed her with calming vibes and soft sing song chanting until Jade fell asleep.

During the night Liz woke several times. She smelled the awful stench from earlier and shivered. Her dreams were filled with pitiful little dogs begging for help. The house had chilled since the wood burner had died down so she put on her warm towelling dressing gown and her woolly slippers before venturing through to the kitchen to put the kettle on. A few handfuls of dry kindling and a couple of logs soon had the fire burning brightly again while she brewed her tea. Roo had decided against coming through from the bedroom. He was still snuggled cosily in his own duvet at the foot of the bed. Setting her cup down on the mantelpiece, Liz took up her Tarot cards and shuffled them, hoping she might learn something of the mystery surrounding her visions. The cards were like old friends and she smiled as she lay them out on the coffee table in front of her. The first card she turned over was The Moon, the card of Illusion, Fear, Anxiety and the Subconscious. Liz nodded to herself. A very fitting card under the present circumstances. The following card was The Star which was a good omen. Liz knew that this card represented Hope, Spirituality, Inspiration and Serenity. A good card to follow one such as The Moon with its prophecy of foreboding. The last card was the 9 of Cups. Liz was pleased. She knew that this card was one of the most uplifting and pleasant cards of the Tarot. Known as 'The Wish Card' it most often meant that whatever you were hoping for would be yours and generally in a short period of time.

Wrapping her cards in their green silk cover and setting them back on the mantelpiece, Liz reached for her cup and sipped her tea. Despite the disturbing visions, she now had faith in a positive outcome. Once back in bed she was soon asleep.

A Little Dogs Prayer Author Jan McCulloch

Chapter Twelve

In the weeks following the loss of my puppies I suffered a mental torture of such magnitude I was barely able to function. I seldom ate or drank and slipped into a strange subconscious world of illusions and hallucinations. In this dream world, I sucked my own flank, imitating my puppies suckling. I sucked until I drew blood. Sean saw me one day and put a large plastic cone around my neck so I could no longer comfort myself. After a few days he removed it because by then I was circling relentlessly and bashing the cone on the bars. He fitted me with a muzzle instead. I scraped my face along the ground and scratched at it with my front paws trying to dislodge it. In my frenzy to get the muzzle off I pierced my eyeball on a sharp piece of rusty wire on one of the kennel panels. I cannot describe the excruciating agony I suffered and in a short time, my eye was infected. I had lost sight in it and it oozed puss. My efforts at relieving the pain resulted in my unintentionally rubbing filthy sawdust into the wound. Sean noticed it   and lifted me by the scruff of the neck to inspect the damage. He sprinkled some sort of powder into my eye and dropped me back to the ground. My eye burned and I ran into a corner quivering in terror. But suffice to say the pain distracted me from my grief.

That night the burning subsided and I felt relief at last. I drank a little fetid water and fell into a restless sleep. I dreamed I was in a strange house. There was a woman with a little dog on a sofa beside a cosy fire. I felt I wanted to go to the woman and I wagged my tail a little but before she could reach down to touch me I woke up. The dream stayed with me and I felt comforted. I hoped I would have dreams like that again.

Sean checked my eye several times over the next few days. I hated how he grabbed me and hauled me up to his face. I hated the smell of him and hated how he dangled me there. My eye didn't hurt anymore but I had no sight in it. Despite his rough handling I was feeling so much better now. There was a new dog in the kennel next to me. The aggressive dog had been taken away one morning. It was dreadful seeing her being lassoed and dragged out with the pole. Snarling and fighting every inch of the way. I don't know where they took her. The new dog was placid and gentle natured and we took an instant liking to each other, laying close together against the bars. I started eating properly again and felt my strength returning.

Some nights I thought I could hear the nice lady from my dream singing in a soft chanting voice. It was as if she was singing in my head. I liked the sound of her voice and often slept soundly after she sang to me.

The warmth of summer brought with it a swarm of flies. Some of my companions leapt and snapped all day at them, driven crazy by the persistent buzzing. Worse still were the dogs who leapt and snapped during the night when the flies were no longer active. These dogs had become obsessively distracted by the flies and could not stop themselves from reacting even when the flies were gone. I shuddered when I remembered the dogs who used to lick the kennel bars and the one who chewed her tail. I had suffered similar obsessive behaviour when I was sucking my own flank after my puppies were taken from me. Some dogs continually circled their kennel. Some leapt silently from side to side until they were exhausted. Few of us escaped the mental trap of obsessive behaviour. We were prisoners in a foul and stinking hell hole. I often thought of my old home and prayed I would return there one day.

A Little Dog's Prayer Author Jan McCulloch

Chapter Thirteen

Morag had been sitting in the shade of the lilac tree by the side of the farmhouse sipping iced lemonade when she heard a vehicle approach. Setting down her glass she rose and wandered into the farmyard to see who the visitor was. Shading her eyes from the sun she was not pleased to see the local Animal Welfare van bumping up the track. Cursing under her breath she took a few steps to the farmhouse door and then yelled loudly for Jock and Sean. The pair of them appeared at a run from the tractor shed where they had been tinkering with their trucks and motorbikes. They stood beside Maw at the farmhouse door and waited in silence for the woman climbing out of the van to come over to them. The dogs in the outdoor kennels barked briefly but fell silent at a word from Jock. They were encouraged to see off strangers but had been taught to be quiet on command.

The Animal Welfare Officer greeted Maw and her sons and introduced herself as Claire Watson, but was met with only a gruff inclination of Maw's head. Her sons stared stonily ahead. They had experience of such visits before. Claire asked questions about a puppy that had reportedly been sold from this very farm and which was currently critically ill in a Veterinary Surgery. Maw growled answers to the questions but Claire knew from experience that these people were unlikely to care about the fate of the puppy. She asked to see the mother of the puppy but Maw grunted that they had sold the bitch last week. Claire would have liked to look around but this family were not about to invite her to do so. Their hostility was palpable. Jock was glaring at her. Sean kicked the ground and cracked his knuckles. After a moments silence Claire sighed and turned to leave. Maw and her boys stood and watched her go.

Maw was unsettled all evening. She sent her boys off to the pub to give herself time to think. Things were getting uncomfortable in this business. She had several dealer friends who had found themselves in hot water with the RSPCA and the Animal Welfare people. Maw knew that she was breaking the law by breeding so many dogs without a license but had got away with it for many years. Maybe it was time to either go legal or give it up and try something else. Neither of those options appealed to her. Firstly, becoming a legal breeding establishment was costly. Secondly, giving up the business just now would be financial suicide. She had nothing to fall back on and her boys were not likely to get employment elsewhere. No, she persuaded herself, there was a third option. Sell up and move to a new area. Another remote farm or smallholding. At least then there would be a few more years of puppy farming before they were under scrutiny again. Pouring herself a beer Maw went to look at farms for sale on the internet. She had no qualms about leaving this farm. She and the boys had only lived here for seven years. Before that they had been in Ireland. And how much easier it was to run a business there!

But at the time they had to make themselves scarce because her boys Dadda had brought big trouble to the door in the shape of drug dealers. She rued the day she had married the great lump.

 He was serving a life sentence for armed robbery. Trying to get enough money to pay the heroin dealer he had fleeced. Oh he thought he was clever that one! He didn't reckon on the dealer coming after Maw and the boys. They had been damned lucky to get out of there alive but the puppy sales had paid off the dealer and she had cut herself and her boys off from their Dadda. Selling their old place and buying the farm, as well as increasing the number of dogs they bred, had worked out very well. But now it was time to move on to pastures new. Maw was confident she would get a good price for their current abode. A farm such as this with outbuildings and land was a developer's dream. By the time her boys piled in from the pub, she had found a place well suited to their needs and had emailed an agent to arrange a valuation of the farm. The only tricky part of this plan was getting the dogs out of the buildings prior to the agents visit. With seventy plus dogs in the kennels now, she was going to have to call in some favours from her dealer friends in the coming week.

A Little Dog's Prayer Author Jan McCulloch

Chapter Fourteen

Despite Jean's best efforts, Jade and Ellie were not getting along together. Ellie clearly resented having Jade back home and would not make an effort to include her in any activities with her friends. Jean was beginning to feel fraught, since every avenue she explored to encourage the twins to be friends drew a blank. She understood how difficult it was for Ellie to have her friends round because Jade behaved so strangely that even Jean herself was embarrassed by her. Jade appeared to be living in a world of her own and only merged with real life when it suited her.

Since coming home, Jade had been to her weekly clinic appointments with Dr Saunders without incident. She was polite, answered questions and generally gave the impression of a normal child. However, Ellie, on Dr Saunders advice, had been taking notes on her sister's behaviour at home, some of which were quite disturbing. It seemed that Jade often talked to herself when she thought she was alone and Ellie wrote in her notebook that Jade would often lay on her bed staring at the ceiling laughing. Jean had not witnessed any of these events but she had noticed a faraway look in Jades eyes and a refusal to respond when spoken to. Jean found herself speaking sharply to Jade to gain her attention.

Dr Saunders entered the notes that Jean and Ellie provided into Jade's medical record each week to refer to over coming months. He was hoping that these strange behaviours would resolve themselves in due course.

Ellie and her friends teased Jade at every opportunity but were disappointed to get no reaction. Jade did nothing but stare at them which eventually became a little unnerving. They would giggle and make faces before running away screeching.

Jade had moved her things into the small box room. She hated sleeping in the same room as Ellie so she persuaded Jean to let her have a camp bed and space to herself. Jean could feel the tension between the twins but could not resolve their issues. Ellie was popular and helpful and doing great at school, Jade was withdrawn, isolated and her school grades had plummeted. Jean was so proud of Ellie and shamefully admitted to herself that she wished Jade could be more like her sister.

Jade was picking up the negativity from her mother and Ellie and despite still feeling the kind and calming influence of her friend Liz every evening in her head, she could not bear to spend any time with her family as it made her anxious and sad. She knew that Ellie was making up stories about her and she knew that her mother was ashamed of her. Each night she tried and tried to talk to Liz through her thought channels but she had not managed to do it. Liz always seemed to know how Jade felt though, which was a great comfort. Jade wanted to see Liz and concentrated hard on her feelings of longing and desire, but Liz always took those feelings to be associated with the loss of Bonnie so she would sing softly and send reassuring vibes. Jade made up her mind to try to contact Liz somehow.

At the next clinic appointment, Jade asked Dr Saunders if she could see the nice lady with the photographs. Jean was puzzled by this request and looked to Dr Saunders for an explanation. He shrugged and spread his palms upwards at Jade and told her he did not know who she was talking about. Jade flushed crimson because she could sense the Doctor was lying. She dropped her head to her chest and refused to co-operate with the rest of the consultation. Jade could not understand why the Doctor was lying but she instinctively mistrusted him now and did not want to speak to him again.

After they left his surgery Dr Saunders rubbed his face and leaned back in his chair with a groan. That damned cleaning woman had a lot to answer for, it was possible the child was going into relapse now and he was sure as hell not going to take responsibility for it, not when he had sent the child home to her mother with assurances that his methods of sedation, therapy and antidepressants had effected a cure.

Once in the car, Jean asked about the lady Jade had mentioned. Jade was agitated and flushed and did not respond. Jean shook her head and let out a long sigh as she turned the key in the ignition. Jade picked up on her mother's frustration but did not feel that she could talk to her about it.

That night in bed, Jade poured out her feelings of anguish and frustration to such a degree that Liz picked up on them and understood that it was important she see Jade. They needed to talk.

A Little Dog's Prayer Author Jan McCulloch

Chapter Fifteen

Dozens of cardboard boxes littered the hall and stairs of the old farmhouse where Morag and her boys were busy packing. Morag sang as she worked. She was pleased she had found the perfect place to continue her business up north and had made a far greater profit on their current home than she could ever have anticipated. Her boys were lugging boxes full of their belongings out to a removal van they had hired from a friend, a rusty old vehicle but mechanically sound. By later today they would be up at the new place, their new beds, delivered last week, already set up on an earlier visit. The fine tuning of moving the dogs was already planned, several groups of whom were being shipped out to board with dealer friends across the country until kennels and pens could be erected at the new farm. Jock was going to stay and supervise the operation the following day. Morag was held in high regard amongst the puppy dealing fraternity so it had not taken much in the way of negotiation. Seven dealers agreed to take ten or eleven dogs each, providing they were rewarded with one or two bitch puppies to add to their own breeding stock.

Jock and Sean hauled out the last of the heavy furniture while Morag checked that Jock had a few beers and a sleeping bag for the night. She was leaving their old beds and other sundry items that had seen better days behind. Her healthy bank balance meant she could afford to replace a few things and still have a tidy sum left over to finance the kennel construction.

Being so busy packing neither she nor the boys had been out to check on the dogs so as the last item was pushed into the removal van she sauntered over to the barn to take a brief head count and jot down the breeds and rough ages of her dogs. She had kept little in the way of actual records over the years but she knew her dogs. She did not altogether trust some of her dealer friends and was determined that they would not get away with the theft of any of them.

In the barn, it took a moment for her eyes to adjust to the dim lighting and the smell was overpowering. She cursed under her breath and took a quick walk along the passageways between the kennels, taking note of which dogs had pups, which were getting too old for breeding and which ones would be the new breeding stock. All the dogs stared at her in silence, their huge eyes unblinking. Some shivered in fear.

Hurrying back to the removal van, Morag gave Jock brief instructions to follow after she and Sean left. She told him that there were two dogs in the far kennel who were too old to pass on or to take with them to breed from so Jock was to dispatch them. Jock nodded curtly. It was easy enough to dispatch a dog, he had done it many times and had a length of lead pipe that he used as a club. He went off to look for it.

As the removal van made its way slowly down the track from the farm, Sean put on the radio and took a swig of fizzy juice from a can taken from a supply in the foot-well, while Morag opened a large bag of jelly sweets to share. They were both comfortably quiet, Morag thinking about the new place and how she would furnish it, Sean thinking about the shapely bar maid in the pub down the road from the new place. He grinned and took another swig from his can.

Back at the farm, Jock had found his lead pipe in the workshop and was making his way towards the barn.

A Little Dog's Prayer Author Jan McCulloch

Chapter 16

Roo was trotting along with his tail waving, looking up at Liz with adoration as they made their way down the street to the village shop. Despite feeling tired having had a restless night thinking about Jade and how to arrange a meeting, Liz was enjoying the walk. The village shop nestled between a row of pretty cottages, hanging baskets bursting with colour beside almost every door. Liz fastened Roo's leash to a hook by the shop doorway and went inside. She only needed milk, biscuits and a few other small items so she was soon waiting in the queue by the counter. It was then that she saw a removal van pull up outside, and at that moment all the hairs stood up on her neck and she heard frantic whispers from the spirits. Liz felt lightheaded but watched intently as two people emerged from the vehicle, making their way towards the shop. Liz gasped when she recognised them as being two of the people the spirits had shown her in the vision, the people from the farmhouse kitchen. She gasped again when she caught a whiff of the foul stench she remembered so clearly from the visions, both from the farmhouse kitchen and from the little dog who had materialised in her sitting room. Liz did not understand the relevance of the stench or the people she was now seeing in the flesh, but she knew that the spirits were urging her to take notice. She stepped out of the queue and began browsing the shelves again while the big woman and her companion entered the shop. From her vantage point by the chest freezer, Liz took in as many details of them as she could. The spirits had ceased their whispering but she could still feel their presence. She allowed the pair to take up their places in the queue before stepping into line behind them. Neither of them spoke but Liz could see flashes of what was going on in their minds by concentrating telepathically on them from close quarters. She shuddered when she picked up the lascivious thoughts the man was having about the young counter assistant, so she concentrated harder on the woman. She caught fleeting glimpses of the old farmhouse, some troubled thoughts about people that the woman did not trust, and then suddenly Liz saw grimy kennels containing small, filthy, terrified dogs. A shiver of icy fingers crawled down her spine when she saw that one of the dogs was the one she had seen in the vision in her own sitting room. Liz almost lost her telepathic link with the woman, such was her shock at the horror she witnessed, but she took a deep breath and held the link a little longer, long enough to see the woman picturing another farm. A farm that Liz knew well, on the outskirts of the village at the end of a long rutted track. It used to be a pig farm in years gone by and still had dilapidated, long low buildings around it that used to be pig sties. But the house itself had been well maintained and had been put on the market a few months ago. Liz stepped away from the woman and released the telepathic link, letting the newfound knowledge settle into place in her own mind.The big woman and her companion bought cigarettes and a few packets of sweets before leaving the shop. Liz paid for her items and was out into the lane in time to see the removal van pull away. Roo was standing pressed against the wall, his tail tucked tightly between his legs. He was afraid of the big woman and her burly companion who had stooped to look at him closely before they climbed into the van. Liz knelt and hugged him close. She could feel him trembling.

A Little Dog's Prayer Author Jan McCulloch

Chapter Seventeen

It had been a strange couple of days. No one had been in to feed us so our stomachs were clenching with hunger pangs. The big woman had been into the barn to look at us all but not given us anything to eat. Soon after that we heard a noisy vehicle depart and for a few minutes only the buzzing of flies and the snap snapping of jaws disturbed the silence. We heard the barn door open and saw the looming shape of Jock walking towards us. Many of us anticipated food and our jowls ran with drool. But then we saw that he carried a weapon and we cringed and crept to the back of our kennels, the cold hand of dread clutching our hearts. Relief flooded through me as he passed by my kennel, moving purposefully to the end of the row. Many of us had witnessed how Jock used the weapon he carried. I saw him reach to open the kennel door at the end of the barn and I turned my face to the wall, trying desperately not to visualise the looks of terror on the faces of the poor dogs he was approaching. But although I could look away, I could not block out the terrified screams or the violent thud of that weapon as it crashed down onto fragile skulls. Jock walked back up the passageway holding two dogs by their back legs, their poor heads smashed in, a trail of blood soaking into the dirty sawdust on the barn floor. We all stared in horror. None of us made a sound that night, not even to snap at a fly or scratch an itch. Our anguish was such that we no longer felt hunger. We felt emotionally bereft, laying there in our own filth with that violent thud still echoing through our souls.

At first light, we heard many vehicles arrive. Loud voices and much laughter echoed through the rows of kennels as Jock brought men carrying cages into the barn. We were lifted into the crates, some of us doubling up to share a cage, and carried outside. The sunlight and the wonderful fresh air was overwhelming, but our pleasure was short lived as we were packed into vehicles lined up by the barn doors. It took our minds of the trauma of the night before but we were anxious and agitated, not knowing what was to become of us. Despite the filth and the stench of the barn, it had been the only thing some of us knew. Most of the dogs had been born and raised here, only leaving the barn to be mated. The younger dogs had never seen the sky or rolled in the grass or smelled the wonderful scents on the fresh breeze stirring the trees. They cowered in shock, unable to comprehend what was happening.

Within a short time the vehicles moved off, one by one. We silently endured the journey, just as we silently endured everything. Confused, hungry and still suffering from the trauma of the night before, we lay shivering in our cages.

At last we reached our destination. Ten of us were swiftly lifted out of the crates and carried into a large grassy, securely fenced area. It was wonderful for me to feel the grass under my paws, and have the freedom to run around after so very long in a small cramped kennel. But some of the other dogs were rigid with fear and did not move from the place they were set down. It was all so alien to them.

There were long water troughs with fresh water. I drank thirstily, the taste of clean water was an absolute joy after the fetid grimy kennel bowls. I took a moment to look at the people who had brought us here. A young couple who, although not affectionate towards any of us, were not giving off any violent vibes as far as I could tell. I gave myself a good shake and then rolled and rolled in the glorious fresh green grass.

That night we were put into clean kennels. No foul sawdust here. Newspaper lined the floors and there was a plastic bed with a blanket. I had forgotten the luxury of snuggling into a cosy blanket. The young couple brought us a meal in a bowl, a tasty meal too. Not cheap mouldy dry food thrown into the dirt. I sat and waited patiently while my food was put into my kennel, and managed a brief wag of my tail in thanks. Once I was settled into my bed I gave a relieved sigh and dared to hope that at last my life had improved a little. As I was falling asleep I heard the calm chanting of the lady I had seen in my dream. She showed me some pictures in my head and I was suddenly alert and up on my feet, panting with excitement. Jade! She showed me a picture of my Jade! I dearly wanted to bark but I dare not chance my luck. The kind lady soothed my thoughts with more chanting and as I settled down again I really did have hope in my heart.

A Little Dog's Prayer Author Jan McCulloch

Chapter Eighteen

When the alarm went off Jean groaned and reached to turn it off. She had not slept well for weeks, convinced that Jade was regressing and at a total loss of how to deal with her. Ellie was such a lovely girl, cheerful and helpful. Jade, in contrast, was becoming more sullen and uncooperative each day. Since the last visit to Dr Saunders, Jean had noticed that Jade seemed to stare into space again just as she used to before she was admitted to the children's ward. Jean sighed and wondered if maybe Jade needed to go back to the Hospital for more therapy. The last thing she needed was for Jade to start self-harming again.

At breakfast, Ellie was her usual cheerful self, chattering about her after school clubs and who had top marks in most subjects in her class (namely herself, since Ellie had significantly improved academically in recent months) but Jade seemed not to hear any of the conversation. She had a puzzled frown on her face, as if she was trying to work out a problem or was concentrating on something. As Jean set a bowl of cereal in front of her Jade suddenly jolted up in her seat, startling the wits out of both Jean and Ellie. A look of joy spread across her features and she leapt to her feet, turned on her heel and raced upstairs.

Ellie and Jean stared after her for a moment, then Ellie pulled a face and tapped the side of her head before grabbing her school bag and heading out of the door. Jean reluctantly went upstairs to Jades box room, not knowing what she would say. She always felt as if Jade could read her mind and no matter how encouraging or positive she tried to be, she felt that Jade could read her embarrassment and shame and negativity as if it was written across her forehead. About to tap on the door, Jean froze. She could hear Jade talking. Not just talking. Giggling, laughing, excited chatter. Pushing the door so she could just see around it, Jean was surprised to see that Jade was laid on her bed with her eyes closed having a completely one sided but very happy conversation. Did this mean that Jade had completely lost her mind? She tapped on the door, gave Jade a moment to respond, then went in and sat on the bed beside her daughter. Still smiling, as if at a secret joke, Jades eyes were alight with a sparkle that Jean had not seen for a very long time. Jean asked what all the jollity was about and for once, Jade did not shut down. She took a deep breath and told her mother that she really needed to go to the village shop after school. Jean, taken aback a little, agreed that Jade could go, but that she, Jean, would go with her. A shadow passed briefly over Jades face before she thought for a moment, grinned, and agreed. Then she was up, racing down the stairs to get her school bag and out of the door.

Jean tidied the girl's rooms and made their beds. She had glimpsed the old Jade. The Jade who was full of fun and laughter. She sighed, hoping against hope that this might be a turning point and that her daughter might seriously be on the mend.

A Little Dog's Prayer Author Jan McCulloch

Chapter Nineteen

Running along to school, Jade felt she could leap into the sky and soar! She had done it. At long last she had managed to telepathically speak to Liz instead of simply listening. And it had happened because Liz had shown her a picture in her head of a poor little dog, filthy and hungry and missing one eye, but never the less it was Bonny! Alive somewhere too. Alive and able to see pictures in her head of Jade. It was like a miracle. Liz had joined the dots and Jade was certain that she would see her little dog again. The shot of electrical energy that Jade felt when she saw Bonny gave her a rush of adrenalin that opened the channels to speaking to Liz through thought waves. They had agreed they needed to meet up and despite her misgivings that her mother would accompany her, Jade was looking forward to seeing Liz after school at the village shop. When she ran into school she was flushed and smiling and everyone stared at her, but she did not care one little bit.

The day seemed to go so slowly, so Jade worked hard and even chatted to a few of her classmates. She ate all her packed lunch, took part in a game of netball and stuck her tongue out at Ellie behind her back which had Ellie's friends in hysterics. Ellie frowned and pulled her friends away from Jade, telling them awful stories about what her mentally ill sister did at home. Jade could read her thought channels and sneakily pushed a picture of Ellie naked into her head, telling her she was going to show it to the boys. Ellie blushed crimson and hurried away, confused at how Jade had done that but far more worried that Jade might carry out her threat. The old Jade was back with a vengeance!

When the bell went, Jade was up and out of school and running as hard as she could. She burst into the kitchen at home out of breath but wearing a huge grin. Jean was pleasantly surprised when Jade gave her a big hug and then raided the fridge. When Ellie walked in, however, Jean could see that she was not in a good mood. She flung her bag down, scowled at Jade and stomped off to her room, returning minutes later changed and ready to go call for her friends. Jade pushed the naked picture into Ellies head again and then fell about laughing at the look of shocked disbelief on her face. Ellie scowled, took a packet of crisps from the worktop and left the house muttering under her breath.

It was only a short walk to the village shop, but Jade was jogging and bouncing along until Jean felt tired just watching her. She still wondered why on earth the shop had inspired such excitement in Jade, but she was quite prepared to follow it through to see what happened.

As the shop came into view, Jade took off at a run and was there, hopping from foot to foot, when Jean eventually caught up. A woman that Jean had never seen before was approaching with a little dog trotting happily beside her.

Jade took one look and raced to meet her, throwing her arms around her in such a forceful hug that the petite woman was nearly knocked off her feet. Jean could see they were both laughing and hugging and laughing some more. Bewildered, Jean tried to apologise for Jade's behaviour but the woman would not hear of it and simply introduced herself as Liz, the lady from the hospital with the photos. Jeans jaw dropped. So, the Doctor lied! She put her arm around Jades shoulders and whispered an apology. Jade just beamed at her. It was wonderful to have people all on her own wavelength at last, even if her mum was a bit slow in catching up.

They all took a seat on the bench by the park across the road from the shop. Liz did not discuss telepathy or tarot or spirits with Jean because she did not feel that Jean was open to such things. Instead they talked mostly about Roo. He loved the attention and enjoyed having hugs too. Jean was puzzled as to how Jade knew that Liz would be here at the shop now, but Liz made light of the fact that she had told Jade in the Hospital that she always gave Roo his walk to the park at the same time every day.

Jade begged that Liz come back with them for tea, and Jean, so relieved to see Jade more like her old self, readily agreed. Liz walked back with Jean while Jade skipped ahead with Roo prancing at her side.

In the kitchen, Jean started to throw a salad together and ushered Liz and Jade through to the sitting room. Jade was glad to get Liz all to herself and the pair of them were soon whispering and giggling together. Jade confided in Liz that she thought she was like the other mentally ill children on the psychiatric ward who heard voices in their heads. Liz smiled fondly at her and assured her that she was most definitely not ill, and that it was in fact a gift that she must use wisely. Jade was a little embarrassed and blushed when she confessed what she had done with the naked picture to Ellie. Liz chuckled and pulled Jade close for a moment. How she wished she had possessed such character when she was a child. Liz lowered her voice and told Jade about the people she had seen in the shop, and how they were moving into the old pig farm at the end of Crab Apple Lane. She implored of Jade to say nothing to anyone, for they must be very careful to strike at the right time. A great deal of planning would be involved before they could confidently make a move. Meanwhile she assured Jade that little Bonny knew they were trying to find her and that she was happier than she had been in a very long time, both because she knew Jade was looking for her and because now people were treating her better than where she had been before. Jade agreed to everything that Liz said, but she found it so hard to quell the excitement she felt giddy and could barely keep still.

After tea Jean agreed to let Jade walk Liz and Roo down to the end of the lane. She also promised to let Jade go to meet Liz after school each day to walk Roo. Jean was secretly thrilled that this gentle, kind woman had become a friend. She felt a warming sense of calm and well-being when in her company. Despite Ellie being sullen when she came in from seeing her friends, Liz had managed to get a smile out of her and for once there had been harmony in the house.

Later that evening Jean put pen to paper and wrote a scathing letter to Dr Saunders, telling him he would be hearing from her solicitor. She smiled as she sealed the envelope. She was certain Jade was going to be alright, despite what the shrinks thought!

A Little Dog's Prayer Author Jan McCulloch

Chapter Twenty

Ordering kennel panels and brackets to fix them, as well as more cheap plastic beds and tin water bowls had taken up most of the morning, but Morag was pleased with the discounts she had secured for bulk buying and moved on to hanging the last of her pictures. She stepped back and smiled at her handy-work. The house was looking just fine. New rugs, a set of fresh cushions on the sofa and a vase filled with daffodils on the window sill gave the room a cosy, comfortable feel. She returned to the kitchen to put the kettle on then went to the back door to shout the boys. They had been fixing doors and shovelling excess muck out of the pig sties in preparation for the kennel panels arriving the next day. Morag was pleased with the effort they had put in and soon had them sitting to the kitchen table, mugs of tea in front of them while she piled bacon and sausages into a large frying pan on the stove. Jock sat idly picking dried blood off his jeans while Sean fiddled about with his phone. The pair of them were looking forward to visiting the local pub that night but they knew they would have to work hard to prepare the buildings for tomorrow before Maw would let them go.

When the boys went back out into the farmyard, Morag phoned round her dealer friends to let them know that she would be ready to take back her dogs within the week. A couple of these dealers made Morag anxious since she had heard stories of their unreliability and untrustworthiness, but she felt that if she made sure they were amply rewarded for their trouble, they would not let her down. She was giving some of them a couple of bitch puppies as payment, but some of them who had legitimate breeding premises licenced by the local council wanted money and charged her an extortionate amount for so-called boarding fees. Pursing her lips, she resigned herself to the fact that she would have to pay up. Indeed, she acknowledged that she herself would have charged a tidy sum should she have been in their position. They were taking a risk keeping a dozen unvaccinated, unchipped dogs on the place.

By late afternoon the boys had finished working on the buildings and were getting showered and cleaned up before having a hearty meal of chicken, roast potatoes and Yorkshire puddings. Morag enjoyed cooking and was impressed with the new stove. As her sons tucked in to their meals, she rolled pastry and lined baking tins, preparing steak pies for the following day. Hopefully most of the kennels would be fixed up by tomorrow evening but she knew she would need to be out there supervising, so steak pie and chips would be a quick and easy lunch. She smiled with satisfaction as she pushed the pies into the hot oven and set the timer.

That night as Morag relaxed with her feet up, watching her favourite television show, she felt a chilly draught tickle her shoulders. Looking round she thought she had closed the sitting room door, but there it stood, open. With a sigh, she heaved herself out of her comfy seat and went to close it.

Pulling the curtains closed and dropping another log into the roaring hearth, she stretched and yawned before settling down once more. A short time later she woke with a start, realising she must have dozed off. Her neck and shoulders were icy cold. She turned to the door. It was open again.

Morag had never been given to flights of fancy but she shuddered and felt a prickle of apprehension. She was certain she had closed the door. It was a good solid door with a strong latch that would not simply open on its own. Yet there it was. Open. Her sons had not returned from their evening out, she was alone in the house. Taking a bottle of brandy from the cabinet in the alcove she poured herself a generous measure and gulped it down before heading off to bed, taking the heavy metal poker from the fireplace with her.

Next morning, rising early, Morag had a twinge of a headache caused by the excess of brandy the night before. She shouted her boys and banged on their doors, gleaning some satisfaction from the thought that their heads would be in a far worse state than her own.

In the kitchen, she opened the oven door to take out the pies. With a frown, she saw they were not cooked. She checked the timer but it seemed to be working fine. With a sigh, she put them back into the oven and turned it on. Shaking her head, she wondered if the stress of the move was affecting her mental ability.

Carrying a steaming cup of tea through to the sitting room, she set about lighting the fire. Reaching for the shovel to take out the ashes, she stopped and stared. The heavy iron poker that she had taken upstairs with her last night was there, sitting in its cradle in the companion set. This time Morag felt a shudder of panic. She was certain she had not brought the poker down with her this morning. She stepped back and sat down on the sofa with a jolt. Piecing together the open door from last night, the unbaked pies, and now the poker, she struggled to make sense of it. But she drew a deep breath and reached for her tea. There was a busy day ahead so she would leave the fire until the evening. Returning to the kitchen she put bread in the toaster and turned to the oven to put plates in to warm. Opening the door, she was aghast to see the pies, unbaked only minutes before, totally burnt black and smoking! Morag decided she needed to call out the service engineer. There was something not right with this cooker.

Out in the farmyard later that morning Morag and her boys worked hard erecting kennels in the old pig sties. The delivery had arrived promptly and after a brief check that they had all the brackets and fixings, the three of them set to, making light work of it between them. Each pig sty held ten small kennels comfortably with plenty of space to hold a dustbin full of dried dog food, wheelbarrow and shovel. By late afternoon they had almost finished and were ready for a good meal. The pies had been thrown in the bin. Morag made sausage and mash and the boys wolfed it down greedily, Sean belching loudly as he pushed his seat back from the table. Jock went to drink his tea but as he lifted it to his lips he looked down and frowned. Swirling the cup, he narrowed his eyes. He felt sure he had seen bluebottles floating in his cup. He went to the sink and poured the hot tea slowly into the sink, but there was nothing. No flies, just a wasted cup of hot tea. Puzzled, he scratched his head and went for a can of fizzy juice instead.

A Little Dog's Prayer Author Jan McCulloch

Chapter Twenty One

Liz had called into the village shop for supplies and was pleased to hear that there was a great deal of speculation about the new owners of the old pig farm. Several local people were chatting with the shopkeeper, so Liz idly looked through the magazine rack while she eavesdropped on their conversation. It seemed that the new folk were having ghostly goings on. They had asked in the shop if the old pig farm was haunted, though the shop keeper had laughed and not taken them seriously. Liz smiled to herself and wondered if her spirit friends were having a little fun.

Later that day Liz met up with Jade to give Roo his walk. They had been careful to keep to a regular pattern for the last week or so, having a gentle walk through the field's skirting the pig farm but not getting close enough to be noticed. Liz told Jade that she had managed to see Bonnie in visions quite clearly over the last few nights and that the little dog was excited about the possibility of being rescued and reunited with Jade. Liz hugged Jade when she saw how tearful she was. The waiting and watching and planning were not easy, but Jade was being brave. She trusted Liz with all her heart.

Their walk took them through a small woodland to the rear of the pig farm. There was a good view of the old ramshackle buildings as well as the kitchen window of the farmhouse. Liz and Jade settled down on an old log and watched quietly, as they had done every afternoon. They had heard raised voices one day, and on one occasion saw a hefty looking youth walking between the buildings, but apart from that all seemed quite normal. That afternoon however, they saw a large van making its way up the lane to the farm, drawing up by the buildings in plain view. Liz and Jade held their breath and crept forward, following the line of a bushy hedge that surrounded the field at the back of the farm. They drew as close as they dared before crouching down in the long grass to watch.

The van driver threw open the rear doors of the van and seemed to be brandishing a thick pole or stick. Liz and Jade could hear him cursing as he was joined by two big lads also brandishing sticks. There was a ferocious snarling and barking coming from the van, then the man hauled on a chain and dragged out the biggest dog Liz or Jade had ever seen. It was a massive animal, with a rough grey shaggy coat. It reared and yanked on the chain, snarling and trying to attack the men who were surrounding it and beating it back with sticks. After something of a struggle, the van driver secured the chain to the rear of the buildings and all three men stood back. The dog paced and circled, snarling. Liz and Jade huddled closer to each other as they watched the fearsome hound lunging and rearing on the chain. Liz took Jade by the hand and they crept softly away, back through the woodland to the village. Roo, who had been quietly by their side the whole time, took off ahead of them, glancing back now and then with a look of concerned urgency. He had not liked the sound of that big dog one bit!

After walking Jade home and having a quick coffee with Jean, Liz took Roo home before taking a pair of binoculars from their place on the hall table. Liz aimed to get a closer look at the pig farm before darkness fell.

By the time she reached the boundary hedge at the far side of the woodland, the big van had gone. Liz could hear the rattle of the chain though, and saw the big dog pacing up and down. The breeze was blowing towards her so thankfully the dog was unaware of her presence. She took out her binoculars to get a better view of the buildings and farmhouse. She could see right into the kitchen. Liz immediately recognised the people inside as the ones from her spirit vision, the same ones who had parked the removal van in the village when she was going to the shop some weeks before. The three of them looked to be having a heated discussion but Liz could not hear what they were saying.

Walking back through the woodland, Liz wondered why the people at the farm had chosen to get such a fearsome dog. She decided it must be for security, to ward off trespassers or nosey villagers. She felt anxious that such a dog was on the premises. However, she was grateful she and Jade had witnessed its arrival, otherwise they may have run into deep trouble if they had decided to snoop around any closer.

When she was home Liz gave Roo his biscuits, made herself a cup of tea and settled down with her tarot cards. Just shuffling them gave her a sense of peace and calm. As she laid them out on the coffee table in front of her however, the peace and calm dissipated as she saw what the cards revealed. The first card, The Tower. She shuddered. Indicating a big (and often abrupt) change, conflict or catastrophe. Liz knew that this card was warning her of sudden and very dramatic occurrences, forces completely external and out of her control. The second card was The Moon. In its normal presentation this card could indicate psychic development, intuition and imagination, but this card was reversed, which meant that psychic ability and intuition would be blocked. Liz frowned. She had not drawn such worrying tarot cards before in her life. She was hesitant to draw a third. Holding her breath for a moment and closing her eyes, she shuffled the cards once more, then turned the third card. The Fool. Liz shook her head. There was nothing practical or sensible about The Fool. But how did his appearance in her spread affect her reading? She sipped her tea and had a dreadful feeling of foreboding. Roo, on the sofa beside her, whimpered and pawed her arm for a moment before resting his head in her lap.

A Little Dog's Prayer Author Jan McCulloch

Chapter Twenty-Two

Morag was furious with her boys. Red faced, lips drawn back in a snarl, she cursed them both for bringing the brute to the farm. It had been Sean's idea. One of his new pals in the local pub had sold him the dog to protect the farm, since so many funny things had been going on. His pals had jeered at him when he mentioned ghosts, they said it was more likely local children giving them the run around. Sean did not like the thought of silly village kids getting the better of him, so he agreed to buy the big dog to keep nosey parkers and troublesome children away. He was a little overwhelmed when he actually met the dog though. He and Jock had never seen anything like it. The size, the ferocity, the pure power and weight of the dog, was terrifying. Sean would never admit it to his pal, but he wished he had not agreed to buy the dog. Jock seemed a little less afraid of it but even so he gave it a wide berth and threw rocks at it when it barked at him. Morag had taken one look at the great slavering beast and saw red. She was absolutely seething. They had taken it upon themselves to get this monster, no permission sought from her. She marched out of the kitchen with their dinner in a bucket and threw it at the dog, vowing to them that she would not cook another single thing until that animal was gone. Red faced, Jock and Sean muttered apologies and promised the dog would go as soon as they could actually handle it. Neither of them wanted the shame of having to tell their pal to come and take it away. Sean rang his pal to ask what the dog's name was, intending to gain its trust. He cringed when his pal told him the dog was called Killer.

The dog did not touch the food that Morag threw at it. Instead, it peed on it and scraped its hind paws through it, spreading it into the mud. Morag stood for a moment looking at the beast. It lowered its head, eyes glowing with malice, a low growl rumbling from its throat. With a shudder she hurried back indoors.

With no dinner on offer, Jock and Sean decided to go down to the village chip shop. Morag had taken great pleasure in eating her own meal of roast pork and all the trimmings in front of them. It would be a good while before she forgave them for undermining her authority.

Killer heard them leave. He sniffed the air to retain their scents to memory. Shaking his great shaggy coat, he stretched and yawned. Scraping a hole in the earth by the wall of the building he lay down in it and rested his head on his paws. He was thirsty but there was no water available. He had been thirsty before. His previous master had withheld water to keep him under control. Killer had followed the dribbling hose pipe like a puppy when he was so parched he could barely walk. Killer had been abused and neglected all his adult life but had never shown fear, despite being beaten and whipped.

As the evening drew in, Killer mooched about on the end of his chain. He cocked his leg on the wall several times to mark his territory then threw his head back and howled. Morag shivered when she heard the mournful song of the wolf. Superstitious folk believed that dogs howled like their ancestors when someone was dying. She peered out of the kitchen window into the darkness, willing her boys to come home.

Killer remembered times when people had been good to him. He remembered being a puppy. His home then, with his mother and siblings, had been full of fun and adventures. His mother was a giant of a dog, an Irish Wolfhound, brave and intelligent. His father was a Caucasian Shepherd, fearless protector of livestock and humans alike. Both his parents had free range of the farm where he was born and he and his siblings enjoyed freedom to run and play. The people on the farm treated them all with kindness. No harsh words, beatings or chains back then. Killer remembered tummy tickles and being petted by the children, two boys and a girl. They had taught him to wear a collar and to sit nicely for a treat. Killer sighed at the memories. Pointing his nose to the sky he howled again.

When Jock and Sean returned from the village, after a skin full of ale from the pub, they heard the howling and threw rocks at Killer, laughing and shouting at each other, Dutch courage and bravado egging each other on. Killer stood tall. He did not flinch or cower away from the missiles thrown at him. He lowered his head, eyes glowing in the dark, and growled. The youths stood and looked at him for a moment, both sobered by the menacing intent of the monster before them, then took themselves inside, slapping each other's backs and making jokes about who would tame the beast in the days to come. Killer settled back into his dug out hollow, his thirst starting to take a firm hold of his attention. He licked the cold stone of the building then fell into a fitful sleep. The creatures of the night went about their business as the big dog slept, one ear half cocked, alert for intruders.

The dawn brought a fine rain. Killer licked the wet stones of the building and found some relief from his thirst. Even licking the raindrops from his heavy coat helped ease his parched throat.

Hearing the approach of a vehicle he barked and leapt on his chain, the frustration of being held captive at all times adding fuel to his guarding instincts. The vehicle slowed and stopped nearby and Killer stood, hackles raised along his back, growling. The occupants of the vehicle gave him a wide berth, making for the farmhouse door. Once they were out of sight Killer yawned and settled back against the wall.

The visitors were welcomed with hot tea and a full breakfast. Morag and her boys were pleased that the first delivery of some of their breeding bitches had arrived safely. Soon be back to business as usual. Four more lots were arriving today, and the stud dogs tomorrow. The kennels had been prepared with the usual sprinkling of sawdust and a wooden pallet in each one. Old pans sourced from charity shops served as drinking bowls and a hose pipe was feeding a water barrel outside.

After breakfast the visitors helped Morag and her boys unload the little dogs, under the watchful eyes of Killer, who stood alert, sniffing the air to catch the scents of the new arrivals. None of them made a sound as they were lifted from their crates and carried into their new kennels. Killer growled deep in his throat when any of the people looked his way.

A Little Dogs Prayer Author Jan McCulloch

Chapter Twenty-Three

I had been looked after quite well in the new place but food was still meagre and no one brushed me or treated my weeping sores. My eye was still very painful and sawdust irritated it. The kennels were cleaner though, and fresh water was always available. Most importantly for me, we were allowed outside into the fresh air regularly, though some of the other dogs who had never ever been outdoors in their whole lives found it an overwhelming experience and cowered close to the ground, shocked and shaking, until they were carried back inside. Myself and the other dogs were still terrified of the people around us and flinched in terror at raised voices or loud bangs but thankfully it was reasonably peaceful here.

My spirits had been lifted since the nice lady in my dreams visited me often, singing softly in my head, promising me that she and my beloved Jade were looking for me. She was pleased that I wagged my tail when I heard her voice and she showed me images of Jade, which made my heart swell with hope and joy.

One day I was brought out into the sunshine and put into a crate in a van. I saw that many of the dogs who had arrived here with me were being loaded too. It made my skin prickle with apprehension and I cowered at the back of the crate. I was afraid that the nice lady who spoke to me in my head would lose track of me if I was taken away somewhere. She must have been tuned into how I was feeling because she crooned softly to me and gave me comfort. I lay down in the crate, resting my head on my paws, and let her soft voice soothe me.

The doors of the van slammed shut, leaving us in darkness. None of us made a sound. The journey was a long one, with no stops for fresh air or to be allowed out to the toilet. Several of my fellow dogs had urinated and it was stifling, our hot bodies packed together. We panted and gasped in the stale air.

When the vehicle eventually stopped, the very first thing I heard made me shake in horror. It was a voice. A voice I knew so well and one which I had hoped I would never hear again. Jock. Shouting and laughing to the driver of the van. I felt sick with dread, and could feel the waves of panic going through the other dogs as we trembled in fear.

The doors opened and the bright sunlight hurt our eyes. Jock was peering in at us, a big grin on his face. Sean appeared behind him with and the two of them chatted to the driver before starting to unload our crates. We all crouched low, paralysed with terror.

There were other vehicles parked up beside the one we were in, and I saw other crates being lifted and carried into buildings. There was a huge dog on a chain who growled menacingly as we were carried past him, but I felt his hatred was for the humans, not for us.

Lifted by the scruff of our necks, we were shoved into our new kennels, the doors slamming shut behind us. I was desperate for a drink but our water bowls stood empty. Slinking into a corner, I huddled on a pallet and felt the weight of desolation creep over me. I could hear the thunderous growls from the big dog outside and wished I had the courage to growl. I dare not even whimper.

Once the last crate was unloaded, the door of the building closed, leaving us in semi darkness. The place smelled strange but was at least cool compared to the van. No one came to fill our water bowls. Thirst is so much worse than hunger, it drove me half crazy. I started to chase my tail in a demented frenzy, which only served to increase my thirst. Exhausted, I lay down and tried to tune in to the nice lady but alas she did not hear me. I felt my mind filling up with memories of my dead puppy, and of my other puppies being taken away from me. I felt the chill of grief settle upon me, a blanket of sorrow that threatened to break my heart all over again. It was then that I heard a new voice in my head. Jade! I sat up, struggling to let the voice in, to let it be clear. Pushing my dreadful memories away I could faintly make out the voice of my beloved Jade, talking to me just as the nice lady had done. At first, I thought the terror and thirst and misery had truly driven me crazy, but then her voice became clearer and I knew she was somewhere nearby. I wanted to bark and leap around so that she would come for me but I knew it was impossible, for Jock and Sean would hear me. I quivered as I sat and listened to her gently saying my name and crooning the soft chant that the nice lady always sang. I dared to hope that I was at long last going to see her again.

A Little Dog's Prayer. Author Jan McCulloch

Chapter Twenty-Four

Jade lay on her bed with her eyes closed, tears streaming down her face. She had at last managed to secure a telepathic link to Bonnie. The emotions she felt from the little dog had almost broken her heart. It had been incredibly hard to get through all the pain and misery but somehow she had done it and had felt Bonnie respond. She lay very still and softly crooned, knowing how soothing this was when Liz had done it for her during her stay in the children's hospital. Once she felt Bonnie relax into sleep, Jade crept from her bed and tiptoed down the stairs. It was almost dark outside so she slid a torch into her jacket pocket as she took it from the peg in the hall. She knew her sister was at a sleep over and her mum was watching tv while chatting to a friend on messenger, so she sneaked out of the house and raced away in the direction of the old pig farm. Her heart pounding with elation and adrenalin, she slowed at the edge of the fields and tried to establish a telepathic link with Liz. There was nothing. She tried again. Still nothing. Feeling that she could not possibly wait any longer, and presuming Liz must be having a nap, Jade hurried up the track between the fields and hid herself by the wood. There were lights on at the farm, and a lot of activity. She saw vehicles drawing away and heard the thunderous barking of the big dog, and the rattle of his chain. Creeping along the edge of the field, Jade dared to approach the farm closer than she ever had before. She hoped that the activity there would mask her approach. The big dog was already barking at the retreating visitors so her presence would go unnoticed.

Crouching only a short distance from the buildings, hidden behind a pile of rusty farm equipment, Jade watched as the last of the people climbed into their vehicle and left. The two big youths she had seen before waved them off then turned to walk towards the farmhouse. In the fading light, Jade saw one of them hurl a brick at the big dog and gasped when it hit the dog with a thud. The dog threw itself towards the youths in a snarling frenzy while Jade crouched lower into her hiding place. There was a loud crunch as the dog leapt forward again, snapping the chain. The youths stood momentarily in shock as the dog bounded forward, then both turned to run. Jade saw their faces clearly in the light from the farmhouse kitchen window, white with fear, eyes popping and mouths gaping. The dog hit the smaller of the two in the middle of his back, the impact sending him sprawling in the mud, screaming. The bigger lad did not miss a step in his haste but shouted back over his shoulder that he was getting the gun. Yelling and wailing but drawing his hands up to protect his head, the fallen youth was being yanked around by the back of his coat, the powerful dogs' jaws sinking into his shoulder.

Although terrified, Jade crept forward from her hiding place and tried to get hold of the loose end of the chain that was dragging along in the mud behind the dog. She slid and lost her footing, but reached out to grab the chain. As her hold tightened the slack, the dog became aware of her presence. There was a heart stopping moment when the dog, fangs still embedded in the youth's shoulder, looked into her eyes. She knelt in the mud, the chain twisted around her hands, a sob escaping her lips, as the dogs focus switched from his victim to her. Killer stood very still. The youth beneath him started to crawl away, not knowing why the attack had stopped but keen instincts of self-preservation motivated his escape bid. He was sobbing and yelping as he went and Killer growled as he wriggled away. Turning his attention back to Jade, Killer stood silently, watching. Saliva and blood dripped from his jaws and he was panting softly after the exertion of his attack. Jade, heart pounding, saw the farmhouse door open and the bigger youth appear with a gun. She struggled to her feet and pulled on the chain, whispering for the dog to follow her. Killer felt the tug of the chain, but it was like the beat of a butterfly's wings against his huge chest. He looked back at the youth on the ground and the other one, trying to pull him towards the farmhouse. Killer growled, but then took a few steps towards Jade. She turned and hurried into the shadows, the big dog following. The chain was heavy and Jade struggled to carry it but the two of them made good progress down the field edge towards the woods.

Jade had a multitude of thoughts careering through her head. She did not like to make eye contact with the big dog despite being glad he had chosen to come with her and not hang around to get shot. She was trying to focus on a telepathic link with Liz but nothing was going through. As they reached the woodland edge, Bonnie pushed into her thoughts, the little dog was excited and recounting her experiences of hearing the commotion outside the building she was trapped in, and being able to smell Jades scent so very close. Jade stopped and looked back. So Bonnie was right there, in those buildings. She dropped to her knees, the weight of the chain and the race along the edge of the field leaving her breathless. The big dog stood close by, watching her.

In the darkness Jade reached into her pocket for the torch and dared to turn it on to help find her way into the woods. The dog was by her side when suddenly there was a shout from behind them and shots being fired. Jade fell flat to the ground, hugging the chain and torch beneath her. The big dog growled but became silent and still when he smelled her blood. She was whimpering and writhing in pain. Killer stepped forward and gently licked the side of her face, laying down close to her so she could feel his warmth and strength. They lay like that in the darkness for some time, the youth with the gun had gone back into the farmhouse. All was quiet.

Jade felt as though her shoulder was on fire. She felt the thick warm blood seeping through her clothes and trembled as the chill of shock crept through her. She was grateful that the big dog stayed close. His loud, strong heart beat and soft breathing were a comfort. Just as waves of nausea were threatening to overcome her, Jade felt Liz right there, trying to establish a telepathic link. Gasping in relief she sent a brief outline of where she was and what had happened before passing out, the pain and blood loss too much to bear. Killer lay close beside her, his head resting over her wound, the warmth of his body keeping the shock at bay.

Back in the farm buildings Bonnie paced the floor of her kennel, sick with worry, desperately urging the nice lady to hurry up and bring help.

In the farmhouse, Jock was pouring a whiskey for Sean who was blubbering while Maw dressed his wounds.

There were deep lacerations to his shoulder and neck and he flinched while gulping the fiery liquid. Maw was furious and glared at Jock, who refused to go back out in the dark in case the savage hound took him by surprise.

Away in her bungalow, Liz was hurrying into her jacket, grabbing a towel and a blanket and a flask of sweet tea she had prepared as soon as she heard Jades cries for help. She took up her mobile phone and headed out of the door, horrified that she had been unable to access telepathic waves from both Jade and Bonnie for some time. The tarot had been right. Liz thought that maybe because Jade had managed to access Bonnie, her own links with them both had been temporarily broken. Hurrying towards the old pig farm, she could now clearly feel Bonnie urging her on, but silence from Jade. Sick with worry she took deep breaths and called upon the spirits to help her.

Once in the woodland, Liz used the torch on her mobile phone to find her way along the path to the edge of the field where she and Jade had watched the activity at the farm over the previous weeks. Her heart stopped when she heard a low rumbling growl. Shining her torch towards the sound, she gasped when she saw Jade, a small, broken bundle, laying face down, covered in blood, with the enormous dog standing over her. With glowing eyes, the dog, tense and prepared to attack, stopped Liz in her tracks. Carefully taking a step back, Liz lowered herself to the ground and sent gentle soothing telepathic waves towards the dog, while asking the spirits to help. The dog stopped growling and took a few steps away from Jade, his expression curious but calm.

Killer had heard the approach of the clumsy, noisy human, and stood ready to protect his new friend. From the moment Jade has grasped his chain he had experienced a flood of pleasant memories from his puppy days, when people had been good to him and children had hugged him and played games with him. His instinct to protect this child was overwhelming. The stranger though was not like other people. He felt her crooning into his head and felt gentle pressure from the spirit world reassuring him with good vibes. He stepped aside and let the stranger tend to Jade.

Liz lifted Jade into her lap and wrapped the blanket round her. Jade moaned and opened her eyes, sobbed a little, then took a few sips of the warm sweet tea from the flask Liz offered to her. Reassured that the big dog was still there, she told Liz what had happened in more detail. Liz was horrified that anyone would shoot a child, but Jade explained that neither of the youths had actually seen her, so must have been aiming for the dog.

Once Jade was feeling a little stronger, Liz helped her to walk back towards the bungalow. The heavy chain dragged behind Killer as he followed them, and Jade wanted the chain to be taken off. Liz was anxious but agreed, shining the torch for Jade to see to unclip it. Upon closer inspection they saw that the chain was padlocked to the collar, so Jade unbuckled the whole thing, with shaking hands, and let it fall into the undergrowth.

Carefully making their way down the street to the bungalow, they were relieved not to meet anyone on the way. Killer walked by Jades side so she could use him for support as well as Liz.

Once home, Liz was horrified to see the extent of Jades injury and immediately called an ambulance. She could not believe the resilience of the small child, her strength and courage in walking all the way back through the woods and fields. Liz called the police too.

But not before hiding Killer in the garage, where Jade asked him to be a good boy and be quiet. Roo was shocked to see this formidable beast in his house, covered in blood but seemingly friendly enough. A far cry from when Roo had last seen and heard him up at the farm.

When the police arrived, Jade told them she had been looking for her dog by the woods when she had been shot by a man at the old pig farm. She did not mention the big dog, or that she had seen him attack someone. She and Liz had agreed that they would protect the big dog at all cost. The police took a statement and then called in reinforcements to go interrogate the occupants of the farm.

The ambulance crew where very kind but firmly insisted Jade be admitted to hospital. Jade sobbed and begged Liz to get to Bonnie as soon as she possibly could. Liz agreed and promised to keep Jade updated on progress. Meanwhile Liz had the daunting task of phoning Jades mother, Jean, to let her know what had happened.

When Maw heard the police sirens approaching, she flew into a rage at her boys. She was convinced that their escaped guard dog had savaged someone. Sean, woozy from all the whiskey he had gulped, staggered off upstairs to his bed. Jock paced the room trying to think what he would say to the police. He was shocked to the core when he heard a loud speaker outside demanding the occupants of the house come outside with their hands in the air. Maw could not believe what she was hearing. But she timidly opened the door and put her hands way up above her head, urging Jock to do the same. She felt sure that her ex-husband was at the root of this, one of his dodgy drug dealing buddies or a false lead had probably resulted in their being implicated. The shock was compounded, therefore, when her son was thrown to the ground, his hands handcuffed behind his back, while he was charged with shooting a minor. Sean, upon hearing the commotion outside, had staggered drunkenly down from his bed and appeared in the doorway, waving a walking stick around, shouting abuse at whoever would listen. A police marksman demanded he put down his weapon. Sean pointed the walking stick at the police man who had his brother on the ground. In the light from the kitchen doorway the walking stick looked like a rifle. The marksman gave one more warning, which Sean ignored, then fired. Sean crumpled down onto the steps of the farmhouse while his brother squirmed in the mud and his mother wailed and screamed in horror.

Liz waited in the woods until an ambulance had driven away, along with five police cars, then she went to explore the buildings. As she shone her torch around the kennels, silent tears poured down her face as she felt the terror and misery from all those little dogs. Tiny prisoners in a hell hole of despair. She soon located Bonnie, who crouched at the back of her kennel until Liz softly crooned to her and she realised who she was. Bonny crawled along the floor on her tummy, wagging her tail but still looking terrified. Liz opened her kennel and took the shaking little dog into her arms. Bonnie snuggled against her and Liz sobbed into her fur. She opened a telepathic link to Jade so the three of them could cry together, tears of relief and joy, then made her way out of the farm and straight to the hospital.

Jade was sitting up in bed, her wounds dressed and her mum holding her hand, when Liz appeared with something hidden under her coat. At the foot of the bed, Liz opened her coat and let Bonnie free. Jade sobbed her name through floods of tears and the little dog crept up and licked her tears. Jades mum, Jean, was speechless. Already having had a shock to find her daughter had been shot and no real explanation for the evenings events, she found herself sobbing too. Bonnie wriggled and licked everyone in turn. Jade sobbed more when she saw Bonnie had lost an eye, and her coat was matted and filthy. The little dog was thin and covered in sores. None of them would ever know the full horror that Bonnie had suffered.

A Little Dog's Prayer Author Jan McCulloch

Chapter Twenty-Five

The following days were a roller coaster of emotions for everyone. Liz had called the R.S.P.C.A in to look at all the little dogs at the farm. A lovely lady from a dog rescue organisation called C.A.R.I.A.D, who specialised in the care and rehabilitation of puppy farm dogs, had made arrangements for each and every little dog to be looked after in foster homes or centres across the country. That week, each little dog had a warm bed, good food, medical treatment and kindness, most of them for the first time in their lives.

After Maw and Jock had been interviewed by the police, Jock was charged with not holding a fire arms certificate, being in possession of a dangerous weapon, and shooting a minor. He was remanded in custody. Maw could not return to the farmhouse as feelings were so high in the village once everyone found out about her puppy farm dealings and her son Jock shooting a child, she feared for her life. Her son Sean was on a life support machine in the hospital. The prognosis was not good. She took a room in a hotel in a neighbouring town, waiting for her own case of animal abuse and neglect to be heard the following week. She secretly feared that at some point the fearsome guard dog who was still on the loose would savage someone and bring even more trouble, but so far there had been no sightings of the monstrous beast at all. Maybe Jock had actually shot it when he fired into the dark that night.

Jade was out of the hospital, enjoying every minute with Bonnie constantly by her side. Ellie was thrilled to see Bonnie too, but was rather jealous that Jade had been involved in a massive adventure while she had been to a boring sleep over at a friend's house. She was glad she had not been the one to get shot though. She was shocked when she saw Jades wound when the nurse came to change the bandages. Despite their differences and the void that had grown between them, Ellie thought Jade was very brave and told all her friends about it, which of course made her the centre of attention at school. She basked in the glory and made an effort to be kind to her twin so that her friends parents praised her, and she basked in the glory of that too.

Liz had managed to establish a firm bond with Killer. She and Jade decided to call him Baron, and he seemed to like the name. Having got him all cleaned up, Liz thought he was a magnificent dog. He and Roo became firm friends. Baron had a huge dog bed in the garage where quite often Liz would find the two of them snuggled in together, taking a nap.

Bonnie was adjusting to life at home again. Raised voices or loud bangs set her off shaking and hiding, but she had been so loved before her ordeal that she was able to fight her demons once she was back with her beloved Jade. She still has moments of great sadness when she thinks of her lost puppies. And nightmares about being in the filthy hell hole. But she is home. And she is loved.

The End

Credits.

To those wonderful people in my life who inspired, encouraged and harangued me. Thank you.

To my Beta readers Denise, Caroline, Liz, Daisy, Martyn. Thank you.

To C.A.R.I.A.D for their courageous and tireless work in campaigning for an end to puppy farming. Bless you.

I would like to think that my book touches the hearts of those who read it. Puppy farming is a very real evil in our society today.

Although a work of fiction, my book highlights the reality of the extreme hardships, horrors and neglect that dogs suffer when they are kept in such conditions. Bonnie would like every single person who reads this book to speak out against puppy farming.

Jan McCulloch

36104874R00035

Printed in Poland
by Amazon Fulfillment
Poland Sp. z o.o., Wrocław